SOME OF WALT WINGFIELD'S LETTERS TO THE EDITOR

ON MEETING HIS NEXT-DOOR NEIGHBOR . . .

"Have you lived in the area all your life?"

He thought about this for a moment, peered at me and said, "Not yet."

ON LEARNING HOW TO MILK A COW . . .

I strove to imitate Don's technique. Matching his determined glare, I took a firm grip on the pail and the stool, strode to Milkshake's side, bent over from the waist, stuck my head into her flank . . .

When I woke up, I was flat on my back some distance away in the straw. The doctor says I'll have two black eyes for a couple of weeks, but there's no permanent damage to the nose.

ON BUYING A HORSE . . .

I've always wanted a quiet horse with some character and I've certainly got that. I can see him in the pasture now. King has a couple of birds perched on his back, just like a dead elm stump. He hasn't moved in over an hour. He just stands there, staring sadly at the ground, as if some great tragedy were unfolding in the ant kingdom below.

ON BIRTHING . . .

My cows are calving, my sheep are lambing and I suppose my goats have got to be kidding.

Dan Needles

LETTERS FROM WINGFIELD FARM

SEAL BOOKS
McClelland-Bantam, Inc.
Toronto

This edition contains the complete text
of the original hardcover edition.
NOT ONE WORD HAS BEEN OMITTED.

LETTERS FROM WINGFIELD FARM

A Seal Book / published by arrangement with
Key Porter Books Limited

PRINTING HISTORY
Key Porter edition published / 1989
Interior illustrations by Robert Johannsen
Seal edition / September 1990

ISBN 0-770-42386-8

PRINTED IN CANADA

COVER PRINTED IN U.S.A.

UNI   0 9 8 7 6 5 4 3 2 1

To Heath

CONTENTS

THE FIRST YEAR

A NOTE FROM THE EDITOR

There's a lot to read in a weekly newspaper. At first bounce, you wouldn't think there was anything much to say about a town like Larkspur. And yet my staff and I manage to squeeze ten thousand words a week into every issue of the *Free Press and Economist*. Forty thousand words a month. About eight fair-sized novels every year, I guess.

Of course, you couldn't find anyone to publish novels like this. That's because we're dealing with the public side of life in the community; only those sanded and polished and varnished facts that can be printed safely without leading to anything more controversial than a brick through the front office window. Nothing is said about the darker side of Larkspur life . . . although we look hopefully every week in the police report.

No. You have to go to the city papers for the juicy stuff. Nowhere in this slag-heap of words will you find the Larkspur resident unclothed, so to speak . . . although I see the Turnip Festival Queen sure made a stab at it this week.

The closest we come, I suppose, would be Walt Wingfield and his Letters from Wingfield Farm. Generally speaking, if you asked my advice on how to run a weekly newspaper I'd say avoid unsolicited contributions. Every crackpot within fifteen miles wants to get something in the paper. But in my case, some of my best material came to me just that way.

Walt Wingfield is an ex–chairman-of-the-board–turned–farmer. He used to be chairman and chief executive officer of MacFeeters, Bartlett and Hendrie . . . the big brokerage house down on Bay Street. Well, one day about a year ago, he gave up his six-figure income and bought a hundred-acre farm out on the Seventh Concession of Persephone Township. He said he wanted to make a stand, to simplify his life.

He'd taken on a tough job. If you look at a climate-and-soil map for this part of Southern Ontario you'll see a small circular zone marked "4A." That is Persephone Township. "Pursefoan" in the native dialect. It enjoys the same climate and growing conditions as Churchill, Manitoba. It is a land of sand-hills, cedar swamp, feldspar outcroppings and about half an inch of topsoil.

The day he arrived in town, Walt stopped by the office to buy a subscription and we had a chat. I could see what he was doing was very important to him. He wanted more of an audience than just his ducks and chickens. He suggested my readers might be interested in a weekly progress report. I listened to him, without telling him yes or no, because I wanted to think about it. He didn't press me for an answer, which surprised me because you know how city people always want to know everything right now.

Then, one day about a week later, I was clearing up at the back after we'd closed and I looked up to see Walt pushing an envelope through the mail-slot. The transformation was remarkable. Gone was the three-piece pinstriped suit and in its place was the "After Dawn" look by Co-op: blue denim bib overalls, a Korean tartan flanelette shirt, brand-new work boots and a green forage hat.

I opened the envelope and found a letter that turned out to be the first in a series of missives that now form a kind of farm diary for Walt's first year out on the Seventh Concession.

Dear Ed: April 21

I was delighted to meet you on my first day in Larkspur last week and I enjoyed our chat thoroughly. You may remember my telling you I've taken over the old Fisher place at R.R. #1, Larkspur, on the Seventh Concession. I've taken a leave of absence from my firm in Toronto in order to try this experiment in farming, which has long been on my mind.

At my age there isn't really much time left for a man to explore some of the things he might have done or been. I've enjoyed some success in the world of finance, for which I'm grateful, but, still, I have a deep and unswerving conviction that a man may pursue his life and satisfy his wants with far less brouhaha than I have experienced so far. Persephone Township is the place to prove it.

The Fishers had their auction last Saturday. I watched as the neighbourhood descended on the place and picked it clean. After it was over, and the Fishers had driven off to their new place in town, the auctioneer walked over the property with me. His name is Freddy. He's an interesting chap, friendly and outgoing, and seems to be well-regarded as an auctioneer despite a very noticeable stammer, which brings his sales to a complete halt from time to time. He runs a beef and dairy operation on the farm next door; plants corn, grain, potatoes, turnips; does auction sales, some blacksmithing, small auto repairs and real estate. It's what I believe is called mixed farming.

As we walked, Freddy and I talked about the farm and my plans for the summer. Although the sun is warm and some green is starting to show through the dead grass, the ground is still spongy, muddy and wet. We stopped beside an old hay-wagon parked out behind the barn.

"That'll come in handy," I said.

Freddy pushed his eyebrows up and stared at the sky.

"Well, now, Walt, maybe I should have mentioned this

before, b-b-but I lent that wagon to old Fisher last summer. You're welcome to the loan of it, if you like."

We walked on.

"What's this? A perfectly serviceable old hay-rake. I'm glad that wasn't sold at the auction."

"Well, now, there again, Walt, that belongs to The Squire across the road. I asked him to take it away before the auction b-b-but. . . ."

I explained that the first thing I was going to need was some cedar posts for a fence.

"By golly, Walt, old Fisher bought some cedar posts off me last fall and n-n-never picked them up. I guess they belong to you now."

"Is there anything else of mine in the neighbourhood?" I asked.

Over the next couple of days I lost the hay-wagon and the rake but I had returned to me: fifty cedar posts, a cream-separator, a cultivator, a set of harrows, five bags of cement, a load of corn and a horse. The horse is a mare named Dolly or something, but I have named her Feedbin since that is where she can most often be found. She's a spirited creature and seems to have been a racehorse at some time or other, because she can turn only to the left. Consequently, I make a perfect spectacle of myself, riding into Larkspur. Freddy has been no help at all about this.

"You'll get used to her" was all he could offer. "Besides, you're not going to be using her much!"

That is where he is wrong, for I propose to teach this horse to pull a plough. As I explained to Freddy, when you drive loud machinery, you miss a great deal of what nature has to offer. You can't hear the rich pageantry of life in the hedgerows if you insist on riding around the fields on a noisy tractor. Of course, Freddy couldn't understand this. But he has been extremely helpful none the less. He put out the word and now all the old horsedrawn implements on the Seventh Concession have been pulled out of driving sheds and left in a pile at my gate. With a few small repairs they'll be as good as new.

I'm not fooling around here. I've never been more serious in my life. I propose to be as good at this farming game as my neighbours, but, at the same time, I plan to preserve some of the old ways. It won't happen overnight, but eventually, the neighbourhood will come to think of me in much the same light as Montaigne and Thoreau were thought of in their communities—gentlemen farmers, rich in barnyard philosophy.

I see myself driving into town in the carriage often enough that they'll feel obliged to put up a hitching post in front of the General Store. Won't that be something?

May 2

I struck the first snag in the livestock department while doing chores this morning. One of my new ducks stood apart from the rest of the flock, rocking uneasily back and forth on his heels, as if someone were trying to push him off balance. When I approached he quacked and fell over, struggled to his feet and went back to wobbling precariously back and forth.

All was clearly not well. After chores, I picked him up and started down the lane for the farm across the road. It seemed an excellent opportunity to meet the neighbours for the first time. By giving them an opportunity to show their expertise and offer advice, I hoped to win new friends . . . and cure the duck.

As it turned out I met my neighbour in the road, a man known in the community as The Squire. He is an elderly man, round-shouldered and bent over from many years of hard work. He was wearing a shabby pair of patched hound's-tooth trousers, which might have been fashionable for a few weeks in the 1960's, and a long-sleeved shirt with pink flamingos on it. He was busy snatching handfuls of bird's nest out of the mailbox and arguing with a squadron of blackbirds hovering a few feet above his head.

"Good morning. I'm Walt Wingfield."

He looked up sharply and peered at me as if the morning sun hurt his eyes.

"G'day."

His attention returned to the mailbox. I made another attempt to start conversation.

"I've taken over the old Fisher place. Lovely morning. Have you lived in the area all your life?"

He thought about this for a moment, peered at me again and said, "Not yet."

I laughed politely and carried on. "I seem to be having a problem with this duck. It doesn't seem to be able to keep its balance. A very bad case of the wobbles, you might say."

That got his attention. The Squire straightened up and examined the duck more closely.

"Wobbles?" he said. "You've kept ducks before, have you?"

I hadn't, but as long as he thought so I wasn't going to persuade him otherwise. "So you think it's the wobbles too, do you?" I asked.

"Yep. Wobbles."

"Well, now that we know it's the wobbles, what happens next?"

"They generally die."

"Yes, but isn't there something we could do before it dies?"

"You could hit it over the head and throw it in the ditch. That'd save you carryin' it back to the barn."

"I mean, couldn't we call the vet?"

"You could do that."

"What's the matter? Is that terribly expensive?"

"No, no. If you got time to carry a duck around I reckon you can afford a vet for him."

The Squire turned and shuffled his way back up his lane. Our conversation was apparently over.

"Appreciate the advice, thanks," I called after him.

I picked the duck up and took him back to the house, set him on the verandah and went inside to phone the vet in Larkspur.

The vet dismissed our diagnosis about the wobbles and said that it sounded more like coccidiosis. He told me to separate the sick ones from the rest of the flock and then add four milligrams of sulphur dioxisol to a litre of drinking-water. I wrote all this down and then asked him what to do with the sick one. His manner changed abruptly and became quite patronizing.

"Oh, is this a small child's pet?" he asked.

"No," I said warmly. "I'm trying to raise ducks for a living."

"I see. Well, give it plenty of water, keep it warm and call me tomorrow if there's any change." He rang off before I could question him further.

I went back out to the verandah to my patient. He was lying on his side now, describing wide arcs across the cement with his foot. I ran back inside and phoned Freddy. You have to hold the receiver down when you dial Freddy's number because we're on the same party line. The phone rang and rang and finally stopped after the tenth ring. I lifted the receiver and heard Freddy's bright "Hyello."

"Freddy, do you know anything about ducks? I have a very sick duck here."

"Now, Walt," he said soothingly, "don't you worry about your poultry. Leastways, not until it's lyin' on its side and kickin' at the air like."

"But Freddy, that's exactly what he was doing just a minute ago."

"Is that right? Well, you run back down there and I'll bet you he's quit that by now. They generally give that up after a bit . . ."

"But Freddy. Something's got to be done. I'm really worried."

"Walter!" he said sternly. "Throw that duck out and get some work done. The forenoon's half gone and you should be ploughin'."

I heard a click and realized Freddy had hung up. I went back out to the verandah and found the duck, stretched out and very still. He was dead. I lifted him up gently, took him down to the apple tree beside the barn and buried him there in a short service attended by a few of his friends, the farm's first casualty.

May 15

Any success I've enjoyed in the world of business has been entirely the result of my habit of setting objectives for myself and my staff. "Fail to plan and plan to fail" is my motto. To keep me on track at the firm, I used a weekly planning calendar that was invented by a successful insurance man years ago. There's room in it for a list of daily things to do, plus what we call the "Dominant" or most important task to be accomplished during the week. I thought it made sense to implement the same system here on the farm because it served me so well at the firm. Besides, I have always believed that a few private-sector principles would go a long way towards improving the farm situation.

Consulting my calendar this morning, I noticed with some satisfaction that the Dominant for week number one —a new fence along the concession road—is done. The Dominant for week number two—a new pig run and a new roof on the driving shed—is also done. However, this week's Dominant—ploughing the top fields—is not done. Now, when this happens, we have a little box at the end of the week that says, "State reason for failure to meet objective." I have noted in this box that Canadian Tire is fresh out of parts for an 1870 chilled-steel Oliver plough, that Feedbin ate her horse collar and that it's been raining since Sunday.

The trick is to stay busy at all times. I decided to drive into Larkspur to ask Ron, the chap who runs the gas station, where I might get a cord of seasoned hardwood for my wood stove.

"Try Delbert Coutts over on the Town Line," said Ron. "You could use the phone in there . . ."

I started into the office.

". . . only Delbert don't have no phone. . . . She'll take a quart, ma'am."

I got back in the car and headed off up the Town Line, thinking I knew where the Couttses lived but in the end I had to stop and ask my way. The driver of the township road-maintainer obligingly stopped his machine, leaned out of the cab and gave me what passes in this part of the country for directions.

"Now, what you do . . . is you go down the Town Line until you get to the old brick church . . . the one that burned down last summer . . . only you don't turn there. You keep right on goin', and when you get to the bridge at the fifth side-road, well, it's about a half a mile before that. So, when you reach the bridge you've gone too far."

Eventually I found it. Two rows of maples lined the drive to a stately Victorian farmhouse, picturesquely surrounded by rusted-out truck cabs, a few rolls of fence wire, a pile of rails, a couple of dead sheep and about fifteen hounds in full cry. I waded my way through the hounds to the door of the summer kitchen and knocked. I assumed the general din would alert any residents to my arrival. There was no response. I knocked again. The hounds were beginning to eye me suspiciously. Just as I was turning to go a small voice behind me said:

"Yes?"

I turned to see a frail old woman peering at me from behind the screen.

"Oh, pardon my disturbing you. Does Delbert Coutts live here?"

"Who?"

"Delbert Coutts . . . does he live here?"

"Oh yes."

"Is he here, now?"

There was a pause.

"No," she said finally.

"Well, where could I find him?"

This was evidently a tough one. Her eyes dropped to the curling linoleum at her feet. My eyes followed hers and I noticed a pair of sock feet sticking out over the edge of an old couch just inside the door. There was no telling who the feet belonged to, and it sure didn't look like we were going to be introduced.

"He's over at the lot."

"Do you mean the wood-lot?"

"No," she said brightly, and we lapsed into another one of those silences she was so fond of.

"Well, which lot?" I was beginning to get exasperated.

"They're building a house . . . over at the lot." This with a motion of the hair curlers to the southeast.

That was good enough for me. I apologized once again for having disturbed her and waded my way back through the hounds to the car. Sure enough, a little farther down the line the frame of a bungalow was rising from a building lot. A man dressed in coveralls sat on the doorstep, having what Freddy calls a carpenter's lunch: a quart sealer of cold tea and a foot-long dill pickle.

"Good morning," I said. "I'm looking for Delbert Coutts."

His response was "Oh yeah," but he didn't say it the way you or I would. He said it in a singsong way, as if I'd said something particularly interesting.

"Ohhhhhhh, yeah?"

"Are you Delbert Coutts?"

"Nope."

I was obviously dealing with a Coutts of some description. Careful use of direct questioning would flush him out.

"Where can I find him?"

"Back at the house."

"Oh no, he isn't. I just came from there."

"Should have been. He was havin' a nap when I left." The sock feet. That clinched it.

"You must be his brother, Alvin."

"Yup."

Finally, I thought, we're getting somewhere.

"I'm looking for cordwood. Maple or beech would suit. I need it in sixteen-inch lengths. Do you have any?"

He studied me thoughtfully for a moment and said, "You got the old Fisher place, don't ya?"

"There's nothing but dead elm on the place and I need something better to burn until the weather warms up."

"Elm burns pretty good."

"I want maple or beech. Do you have any?"

He screwed up his face, shook his head slowly and stared at the ground. I prepared for the worst.

"Yup . . . some."

"I'll give you thirty dollars a cord."

"We been gettin' thirty-five."

"Delivered?"

"Could do."

Now normally, I wouldn't conclude business on such flimsy evidence that the wood did indeed exist, that they had a truck or that there was the slightest chance of seeing it delivered before September first, but I pressed on. I pulled a roll of bills from my pocket and peeled off a ten, a twenty and a five and handed them to him. Judging from the expression on Alvin's face, either he had never seen folding money before or he had no idea that business could be conducted at such breakneck speed. It couldn't be helped. I didn't want to spend the whole of week number four out there.

On my way home I stopped at the gas station to ask Ron what on earth was the matter with those people. He was deep inside the engine of a Dodge pick-up and he listened as I told him my adventures with the several members of the Coutts family. At the end of the story, he emerged from the engine compartment, wiped his hands on a greasy rag and pulled his cap around straight.

"Funny thing about the widow Coutts," he said. "She seems to have gotten mixed up about those boys. Sometimes she can tell them apart same as you or me. Other times . . . heh! Try her now, Willy," he called to his client, who was sitting behind the wheel of the Dodge. The engine turned over in a series of dry heaves, caught and revved up to a rattling crescendo.

"One thing about them Coutts people though, Walt," he shouted over the din. "They sure are good at getting you to figure things out for yourself. Like most folks around here. You'll get used to that, Walt."

An explosion rattled the windows of the garage and a sheet of flame shot up from the truck carburettor.

"Whoooaaaa JEEEZ! Shet her down, Willy!"

I ducked out the side door and went home to wait for my load of wood.

May 25

As soon as the sun breaks over the hill, the chill leaves the air and the land springs to life. Bees hum in the ancient fruit trees like the Toronto Symphony warming up. This morning, I walked out to get the mail along a cordillera of fruit blossoms, drinking the air as if it were the finest champagne. For the first time I realized the extent of my inheritance. Apples, pears, a few black cherries and, right smack in the middle, for no apparent reason, a great big mulberry tree. I was looking at the earliest phase of a mulberry pie.

I tried to imagine how old these trees must be. A hundred years? What stories they could tell about this land and the people who farmed it. I walked in a wide circle through the trees, towards the mailbox, soaking in the first real warmth of spring and thinking how far away from gridlock; fern bars and smog I have come in the last six weeks.

"And this our life, exempt from public haunt
Finds tales in trees, books in the running brooks . . ."

"G'day."

The scratchy old voice startled me and I looked around to see The Squire, who had been leaning against his mailbox and watching me stumble through the orchard, reciting poetry to myself.

"Good morning," I said.

"Nice fence."

I thanked him for the compliment and showed him what was to come. Within a few days there will be cedar posts and eight-strand wire going all the way down the concession to the corner of the side-road.

"Won't be the same without Fisher's cattle down my lane all summer," said The Squire, with a chuckle. "I may keep a garden this year."

"Well, one thing I can promise you is good fences," I said stoutly.

He squinted critically at my fields and nodded his approval. "Yep. I can see you're takin' a real interest in the place. It's a good farm. Just needs to be brought back a bit. I've often thought how you might make this farm pay."

Now, here was the advice I was looking for and it looked like we were going to hit it off after all. I settled back and prepared for a good chat about crops and the weather.

"You have?"

"Oh, yeah. Now you take this here field. The first thing you want to do is square it off, right back here to the lane." His arm made a chopping gesture right through my orchard.

"Square it off . . . ?"

"Then you get on 'er with a trencher crew and tile 'er up. Three rows to the corner down there. She'll drain like a bath-tub . . ."

"But you don't mean these trees here?"

". . . then you bulldoze that hedgerow out there right the way back to the road."

"But you can't be suggesting I get rid of the orchard?" I protested.

"Well, of course. You gotta get rid of them old trees."

"But they must be over a hundred years old!"

"I know. It's a dirty job, wrestling with those old brutes. But I'll give you a hand. A couple of days with a chainsaw and a back-hoe and you'll see the back of 'em."

I thanked him politely for his offer of assistance but explained that I planned to keep the orchard.

"What for?" he demanded, a scowl returning to his face.

"Well, there must be some money in apples, don't you think?"

"I expect there's a lot. No one's got any of it out yet."

I felt I was missing something. "I know I'm not going to make a fortune," I said. "But there isn't another apple-grower within five miles of here."

"They're all dead. Starved to death tryin' to grow apples at ten cents a pound. Look here, Mr. Wingfield. You can't make a farm pay by wastin' your time and wastin' your land. But you go ahead. You doctor up them old fruit trees if you like . . ." He turned away to leave, paused and looked back over his shoulder.

"Give you a place to run your ducks, I expect."

And he shuffled away, back up his lane.

I walked back to the house, feeling completely deflated. It had been such a beautiful day and it was spoiled by a grouchy old man who didn't like trees. I banged the garden gate so hard it jumped off its hinges and toppled over onto the paving stones. I looked back up the lane to The Squire's and fumed for a minute. He was walking up the gangway of his barn, towards the open mow, and I could see him framed in the daylight shining through from the east because several barn boards had blown off the far wall. A few pieces of steel were missing off the roof, too. In fact, the whole farmstead had a decaying look about it.

He's certainly managed to disguise his own prosperity. What does he know about making a farm pay, anyway? I looked at the fruit trees again, took a deep breath of perfume and pollen and made a decision.

These trees can stay right where they are.

June 2

Writers who describe night-time in the country are forever rattling on about the chirping of frogs and the rustle of night wind on leaf. They've obviously never been around here on a night when the moon is full. The sound I most commonly hear is the scream of some unfortunate creature being mugged at the back of my swamp. Last night, the hounds got the scent of a coon or something, chased it around the quarry for about an hour until it made a break across the top of the hill, and then finally treed it up by Freddy's. A stream of lanterns issued from Freddy's, danced across the top of the hill, and the air was shattered by a volley of artillery that sounded like the opening of the spring offensive.

From where I lay, I could practically hear the whisper of little wings as another furry soul wended its way heavenward. I was just managing to get back to sleep when I heard a sharp "Hyello" from downstairs. Wondering who it could be at that late hour, I got up, stumbled downstairs and opened the door.

There I saw a face peering at me from the other side of the screen, a great, pale, cavernous face with hollow, sunken eyes and a stained roll-yer-own hanging from the lower lip. For a moment I thought someone must have propped a dead man at my door as a horrible practical joke. I felt along the wall for the axe.

"G'day, Walter," said the corpse, only his lips didn't move. Then I realized the voice belonged to another man, out of sight behind the door. It was Freddy, slightly unsteady on his feet, glassy-eyed and grinning cheerfully.

"I was wondering if you m-m-might have a drop of lemonade, Walt," He teetered back on his heels and came forward again. "Jeez, I hope we didn't get you up."

I let them all in. There was Freddy, his two nephews, Willy and Dave, who had to stoop to avoid hitting their heads on the door-frame, and the corpse, who turned out to be Jimmy, the hired man. Hired for what I don't know. He looked to be thirty years past his retirement.

It was only polite to offer them something to drink and, of course, I joined them. I really had no intention of sitting up to all hours, but then, this was the first company I had had for six weeks. I'm a bit fuzzy about how they talked me into it but soon we were all sauntering back up the lane towards Freddy's, for a nightcap.

Inside Freddy's kitchen, caps were snapped off beer bottles, chairs tilted back and sleeping hounds nudged aside for more foot room. The house had an odd smell to it: stale beer, kerosene lamps, wood-smoke and dead mice. Willy and Dave look like two straggly Fenians and they laugh like guinea hens at just about anything you say to them. It's a high-pitched laugh that carries for miles and travels through house walls undiminished.

They were talking about some horse they were thinking of taking on the winter racing circuit through the States.

To contribute to the conversation I turned to Jimmy and asked him if he had much experience with horses. This produced an immediate effect on the company. Willy and Dave swung their chairs around and made an elaborate display of getting themselves comfortable.

"Tell him about the big bay mare that ran the lights through Larkspur. Heeyah, heeyah!" said Willy.

"No, no!" said Dave. "Tell him about the black trotter that ran away with you and Violet McKeown on the way up the Pine River to church. Heeyah, heeyah!"

Jimmy reached out with his long waxen fingers and delicately brushed the ash off his cigarette into the cuff of his pant leg. "No," he said, in a gentle quavering voice with a trace of an Irish accent. "There's a story in both them harses, but I'll tell yas about the pair of matched Clydes I bought off old Ewing, the year after the war."

"Which war was that, Jimmy?" asked Dave. "The one against the States?"

"No, no, of course not," scoffed Jimmy gently. "The Fourteen-Eighteen War." Turning to me he continued. "Old Ewing, Walt, he had a hell of a temper. And these harses, ahh, they was a balky pair of brutes. One time they balked real bad on him when he was drawing straw just up the line here. Well, he got off the wagon and he flayed 'em with the lines until his arm damn near wore off. But they wouldn't move. They just quit."

"So what did he do?" I asked.

"He reached up and he pulled an armful of straw from off the wagon and he threw it down there right underneath the harses. And then he set fire to it, so he did. Well, the harses jumped ahead, about ten feet. Then they quit again. Then the wagon caught fire, and old Ewing had to cut the harses out of the harness to save them, and the wagon burnt right to the ground, so it did. Right to the damn ground."

I was just going to say it served the fellow right when Willy broke in.

"And the straw, Jimmy, did the straw burn to the ground, too? Heeyah, heeyah!"

"Well, of course it did."

"And old Ewing, Walt," said Dave, "he had two wooden legs. He burnt to the ground, too! Heeyah, heeyah!"

A beer bottle bounced off the wall by Dave's head. Freddy rescued the situation by getting Jimmy to tell some more horse stories, but Willy and Dave had heard them all before, and soon Jimmy's face looked longer and sadder than ever. When I made an attempt to show interest Jimmy embarked on the story of his life.

He came from a small town outside Galway in Ireland. He had a childhood sweetheart and, after he'd finished his apprenticeship, they were able to be married. The very day of the wedding, however, his bride "took a fever." Jimmy saddled up the mare, rode all the way into Galway to get the doctor and brought him back. He waited in the kitchen while the doctor went into the bedroom. A short while later, the doctor came out, laid his hand on Jimmy's shoulder and said, "She's gone, Jimmy. Flossie's gone."

Jimmy never even went into the bedroom. He gathered up a few belongings, got back on the mare, rode into Galway, got off, sold her and bought himself a steamer passage to Canada.

The room was very quiet when Freddy finally spoke. "Sing it, Jimmy . . . sing it to us."

Jimmy cleared his throat, tilted his head up and began to sing in a distant and tremulous tenor:

"If you ever go across the sea to Ireland
It may be at the closing of the day
You will sit and watch the moon rise over Claddach
And watch the sun go down on Gal——"

But he didn't finish. Tears choked him on the last phrase and he sat there, silently shaking his head in apology. It was all too awkward and I looked away. I thought of the years of loneliness and hopeless labour this man had put into the stony fields of a strange land and it filled me with sadness.

When I looked back . . . they were all asleep.

I got up, went out onto the verandah and thought about going home. The moon had gone down and the night was inky black and quite cold. I could just make out the shadowy shape of trees around the house and, far off down the lane, the distant lights of my own house. Groping down the lane in the dark without a light was out of the question. The screen door creaked behind me, and I turned to see Spike, one of the hounds, squeezing his way out to join me.

"Hello, Spike," I said, rumpling the loose skin on the back of his head. "You sober, too?" I found myself suddenly sitting on the verandah and realized I wasn't quite sober either. Obviously, I was there for the night, what was left of it. I picked up a couple of chunks of wood from the verandah and took them back into the kitchen with me, made a quiet fire in the wood-stove without disturbing the sleepers and curled up on one of the old chesterfields.

When I woke up, I was alone, except for Spike the hound, who was draped across me like a throw rug. A light morning fog crept in over the window-sill. It was cold, my head ached and, even with a stuffed nose, I could still smell stale beer, kerosene, wood-smoke and . . . smoke, lots of smoke. Down the hallway a thickening grey cloud hung along the ceiling.

"Freddy!"

An answering groan came from the verandah. I dashed out to find Freddy curled up on a old church pew.

"Freddy, wake up! There's a fire! It's upstairs, I think!"

"Mm?" said Freddy. "Ah Jeez, not again!"

Freddy grabbed an old hoe handle and started beating on a steel rain barrel beside the verandah.

"Everybody up! We got a fire!" he yelled.

Things started to happen fairly quickly after that. Freddy's fire alarm had the same effect on the household as a swift kick to an anthill. Seven people I hadn't even met came out of side rooms. Jimmy staggered out, clutching a case of beer he'd rescued from under the kitchen table. A bucket brigade quickly formed; Dave manned the pump, Willy and Freddy raced back and forth, carrying pails of water up the stairs. They didn't search for the source of the blaze. When they reached the top of the stairs, they would kick open a bedroom door, heave the pail contents in on the floor and run back downstairs for more. Jimmy stood by the pump, snapping the caps off beer bottles and handing them to the fire-fighters.

"It's a damn shame they can't see us," he said wistfully.

"Who?"

"Why the neighbours, Walt. Look at the job them boys are doing. It isn't fair."

"What isn't fair?"

"Why, they could put the fire out and save the whole house and people would still say we were drunk." He shook his head sadly and bent to fetch out another bottle of beer.

I turned to see a pick-up truck coming down the lane at full speed. It was my neighbour to the south, Don the dairy farmer. Word was spreading quickly. Within the space of half an hour, the whole of Larkspur had heard about Freddy's fire, except the fire department. The place began to take on a carnival atmosphere. Cars lined the lane both sides right out to the road; children bounced up and down on chesterfields we'd dragged out onto the lawn and the ladies organized a lunch table for the volunteers. Eventually the fire truck arrived, skidded to a halt in the turning circle in front of the house, lights flashing and radio crackling. Moments later a fireman emerged from the front door of the house.

"Someone lit a fire in the wood-stove," he said in a stern voice. A great sigh went up from the crowd. I stepped forward and raised my hand.

"I did. It was cold and . . ."

I heard my words echoing among the seventy-five people present.

"He lit a fire in the wood-stove . . . he lit a fire in the wood-stove . . . he lit a fire in the wood-stove!"

Freddy came over to me, shaking his head wearily.

"Walt, there's no s-s-tove-pipe above the ceiling. We took it out after the last fire, when we put in the gas furnace. J-j-jeez, Walt. Everybody knows that."

I felt my face achieve the rich crimson of a Persephone Township sunset.

"Send me the bill for the damages," I said. There was nothing else to say. I left.

The morning did have one positive result. Apparently, I now own a dog. Spike the hound followed me home over the fields from Freddy's without so much as a backward glance. He's been asleep in front of the fire ever since. I think Freddy's fire was the last straw for him. He's come here looking for some peace and quiet. I've decided he can stay as long as he likes. He's of an age now when he's no longer a danger to wildlife, and besides . . . he admires me.

He's probably the only one left who does.

June 10

This isn't working out. Not at all the way I planned it. The book says that if you live in Zone 4A, you should have your spring planting done by June the tenth. Here it is and I haven't even finished ploughing yet. I finally got Feedbin and the new horse, Mortgage, harnessed together and ploughed a few wiggly furrows. But Feedbin turns only to the left and Mortgage must be Australian, because she turns only to the right. Then it clouded over and dropped about a foot of rain in the space of half an hour, with the result that my field now looks like Vimy Ridge.

I never realized what an opportunity there is in farming to make a complete idiot of yourself in public. Sitting here under the maple tree at my line fence, I have a perfect one-hundred-and-eighty degree view of failure on all sides. On the way down the Seventh Line you drive by field after field of beautifully manicured spring oats and barley. Then you get to my place. Cars stop and whole families get out to take pictures of the mess.

The people really are wonderful around here. I can hear them now down at the General Store in Larkspur, laughing and telling each other what a mess I'm making of the old Fisher place, trying to plough with horses.

There is absolutely no way to please them. If I had a half million dollars' worth of farm machinery like my neighbour Don, they'd say I had more money than brains. If I hired one of them to work the fields for me they'd say I was lazy. If I had a four-year degree in agriculture like the McKees' oldest boy, they'd complain about all book learnin' and no common sense.

The only way I could possibly please them would be to arrange somehow to have myself born here fifty years ago and then do everything exactly the way I did it last year. Which is fine for them; they're the only people I know who can lose money thirty years in a row and then move into a big house in town for their retirement.

In the middle of all this I got a letter from the new chairman at MacFeeters, Bartlett and Hendrie . . . my old partner Alf Harrison.

Dear Walt:

The investment community has accepted the news of your departure and the company still survives. This letter is not intended to persuade you to come back. I know when your mind is made up. But if you can't be reasonable, I will try to be for you.

You can play Farmer Brown for a year and we'll keep your name on the letterhead. If at the end of that time you decide to come back, no questions will be asked, no explanations required. In the meantime, I haven't told anybody about your determination to farm for a living. There's no sense ruining your reputation over this thing. I've just told them you're being treated for a drinking problem.

My best wishes to you in this colourful and exciting new venture. I remain,

Yours sincerely,
Alf

Clearly, I am disappointing people on all sides. But that's too bad. I may only get one acre ploughed, and it may not sprout till Hallowe'en, but at least it will be my acre and my crop.

Or so I thought until this morning. I was just preparing to harness the horses for yet another attempt at cultivation when the air around me was filled with the sound of engine noises. I looked up to see my neighbour Don approaching from the south on his big articulated Minneapolis Moline diesel tractor, pulling an eight-furrow plough. He swung in my gate and, without stopping, headed straight into the Vimy Ridge field and dropped the ploughs.

I yelled at him to stop. I shouted at him to get that tractor out of my field. He wouldn't listen. I chased him around the field twice, telling him what I thought of charity and modern machinery. He paid no attention at all and ploughed the whole field in less than an hour. Willy and Dave turned up with disks and cultivators, Freddy brought harrows and a seeder, and Jimmy and The Squire came just to pick stones. At one point there were five tractors in my field, whirling around at top speed, as if I wasn't there. The crop was in before dark.

I suppose I could have been more civil about it. They were only trying to help. But it left me feeling like a complete failure and I found it difficult to stand there and watch them make a mockery of my efforts to hang on to the old ways.

After they all left, Spike and I went down to the pond to sit on the dock in the dark. We just sat there in the cool night air, watching the little trout jump at mayflies and listening as a halting version of "Stardust" drifted over the fields from Don's verandah, where he sat playing his old trumpet. Up at Freddy's, it sounded like another coon hunt was being organized. It was one of those early June nights when you can actually hear the crackle and pop of things growing around you. We just sat there, not saying anything to each other, until finally, Spike said "Woof" in a conversational way. There was a rustle in the grass and we looked up to see The Squire standing over us.

"G'day, Walt."

Spike moved over a few feet to give him room to sit on the dock. We talked about this and that for a few minutes before we got around to the events of the afternoon.

"You see, Walt, there's just one deadline in farming that you don't mess around with and that's the spring planting. Now, me and the boys were content to let you . . . experiment with them horses so long as you didn't go past June the tenth. But come today and no sign of a crop, well, we did what we had to do."

"Why the hell do they feel they have to look out for me? Do I appear to be some sort of invalid?"

"They wouldn't want to see you stuck, Walt."

"That's extremely noble of them. But where I come from, a man is allowed to fall flat on his face if that is what he wants to do."

The Squire nodded and got to his feet. "I figure they'll leave you enough room for that, Walt." And he disappeared into the darkness.

"Woof," said Spike, looking at me with a straight face.

"Woof yourself," I said, and we went off to bed.

July 1

I have finally realized a long-held ambition and become a dairy farmer. This week, Don and I drove down to Wychwood where a friend of his runs a story-book dairy farm, complete with herds of cuddly brown Jersey cows. Don picked out four flabby old girls who were used to being milked by hand during power failures and we loaded them onto the truck. I thought we should have at least one younger animal, to diversify the portfolio, as it were, and pointed to a young heifer that had just freshened.

Don and his friend didn't exactly object, but I'm beginning to catch on to these characters now. They just stood there stroking their chins, and said, "You could do that," which, translated, means "Only a real idiot would do what you're about to do."

We got the registration papers for all of them, showing the sire and the dam, the sire of the sire and the dam of the dam, and they all had the most precious names—impossible titles such as Acme Heritage Shady Grove Apple Blossom and Jester Generation Emperor Fred. The first thing we did when we got them home was give them some real names: Lollipop, Cupcakes, Creampuff and Yoghurt. The little heifer we named Milkshake.

Don stayed to help with the first milking, showed me the basic rules of sanitation, measured out the required portions of sixteen percent dairy ration and demonstrated the art of stripping a cow of milk in about seven minutes. The old girls stood very quietly for all of this; then we got to Milkshake. She's a shy, delicate creature with a deep dish in her forehead and eyes that stand out like those of a frog underfoot. She evidently views the milking process as a form of indecent assault. Don showed me the correct approach.

He's an ex-welterweight boxer, with broad shoulders and a solid build. He fixed Milkshake with a determined glare, took a firm grip on the pail and the stool, strode to her side, bent over from the waist and then stuck his head into her flank just below the hip-bone. A brief struggle ensued, but the heifer was effectively pinned to the wall by Don's stance. He got the stool underneath him and, within a few minutes, he was milking away quite successfully. He milked out the back quarters, straightened up and handed the pail and the stool to me.

I strove to imitate his technique carefully. Matching Don's determined glare, I took a firm grip on the pail and the stool, strode to her side, bent over from the waist, stuck my head into her flank . . .

When I woke up, I was flat on my back some distance away in the straw. The doctor says I'll have two black eyes for a couple of weeks but there's no permanent damage to the nose.

Milkshake is back home in Wychwood.

July 25

I was trying out the team again in a fairly simple exercise with a stone boat this morning. Since it has no tongue to break and no moving parts of any kind, I thought it would offer good training at low risk to life and property. But within ten minutes we had worked up to a level of excitement worthy of the Calgary Stampede. So I put both horses on report and went up to Freddy's to pick out an older, more experienced animal, before it went to Owen Sound for glue production.

Freddy and I leaned against the corral fence and I watched the herd mill by as Freddy listed the track record, pedigree and hoof size of any individual he thought might appeal to me. They were a pretty nondescript lot, but Freddy's patter buffed them up a bit.

"Well now, Walt, you see the big chestnut mare there? The one with one ear, yeah. You see the way she holds her head? What a stride! Don't pay any attention to that bit of mange over the withers, Walt. That'd clear up with the sun on it in no time. And you see that two-year-old? He'd make a dandy hunter . . . with a little work. You could have him registered, if you want."

In Freddy's eyes, any horse who can stagger onto a truck unassisted can be registered. A big colt lumbered by.

"That fella's mother was a thoroughbred . . . and his father was half quarter-horse."

Great, I thought, That would make him seven-sixteenths dog food.

"Sure, he's ugly," said Freddy, with his auctioneer's gift for perceiving silent scepticism. "Most yearlings are. But strong, you know. His mother won a couple of races at Woodbine. I've half a mind to take that young fella and race him myself. There's a lot of money in him, if you bring him along right."

Despite the brilliant future ahead for this colt, his price was the same as the rest: a hundred bucks.

"You're lookin' for somethin' heavier, are you? To draw, like? Well, come on inside and I'll show you old King."

Freddy opened the barn door and we stepped into the gloom of the stable. It was cold and damp and the air was heavy with the smell of horse, harness and hoof paint. Half-way down a row of hefty Holstein cows, a huge black work-horse towered fully three feet above the rest of the animals. Only the shoulders and hindquarters were available for viewing. The head was out of sight somewhere at the bottom of the oat box. It looked like a great big, black grand piano on edge.

As Freddy listed the options on this animal I began to wonder if he came with a head. I reached out to touch him on the flank and an enormous head rose up from the oat box and turned to look at me. For a moment, I felt as if I was looking into the eyes of some ancient priest of Shangri-La. In those luminous brown pools I caught a glimpse of yesterday, before the milk wagon, before the prairie schooner . . . even before King Arthur's court. This was a very old horse.

"Hullo, King," I said.

The head returned to the oat box.

"I guess this fella would be old enough to vote, Walt," said Freddy, edging up beside the horse to undo his halter. "But strong. As long as these fellas keep their teeth, they never quit. You fit him up with a set of dentures and he'll last you another twenty years. Hyep!"

Freddy leaned over the oat box and spoke very distinctly into King's left ear as if he were speaking into an apartment intercom.

"Back up, King. Back up."

I understand that the pilot of an airliner has to wait seven seconds after applying the throttle before the engines respond. It was the same with King. The head rose up from the oat box, a blast from the nostrils filled the stall with a fine spray, one enormous hoof rose and came down almost tentatively on the cement walkway. Joints cracked, bulk shifted and King was underway.

There is something very impressive about a really big horse. I remember when I was a kid going down to the Royal Winter Fair in Toronto and watching the big Belgians and Clydesdales line up for their events. I remember most of all their huge soft noses, big kind eyes and hooves the size of dinner plates that came down on the concrete with a clank you could feel through the soles of your boots twenty feet away. I can't say I ever dreamed of owning one; they seemed so impossibly big and far away. But I did dream of having one as a friend some day, to go and visit.

Once he was out in the sunshine, I could see that King was a far cry from those sleek bob-tailed Belgians and Percherons with their nickel-plated harness. But the eyes and the nose and the dinner plates . . . they were all there, all right.

"A hundred bucks, Walt," said Freddy.

Same as the rest. And so I led old King down the Seventh Concession, his great chipped hooves scraping along and his nose barely three inches off the ground, blowing up little hurricanes of dust every few steps. I opened the gate to the pasture, unsnapped the lead rope and gave King a slap on the rump as he plodded by me into his new home. The look he gave his new pasture-mates, Feedbin and Mortgage, was one of unspeakable weariness, as if he had seen so many pastures and so many pasture-mates that all sense of novelty was hopelessly lost for him.

I've never seen Don laugh so hard. I didn't expect Don to see what I see in King. But then, I didn't expect him to tell me that I could have saved a hundred bucks by throwing a horsehair rug over a rail fence and emptying the wood-stove ash bucket over it. The reaction elsewhere in the neighbourhood has been much the same. King's age has been estimated at somewhere between eighteen and fifty-five and his pedigree judged to involve Percheron, Clydesdale, Belgian, musk-ox or woolly mammoth . . . take your pick. But I don't care. I've always wanted a quiet horse with some character, and I've certainly got that.

I can see them all down in the pasture now; my herd —Feedbin, Mortgage and old King. King has a couple of birds perched on his back, just like a dead elm stump. He hasn't moved in over an hour. He just stands there, staring sadly at the ground, as if some great tragedy were unfolding in the ant kingdom below.

This place gets to look more and more like a farm every day.

August 1

The step down from the barn floor to the ground is quite a jump for a man my age. Don and I made the hop in the dark last night and I went over on my ankle.

"Are you all right, Walt?" asked Don, holding me up by one arm.

I put my weight on the foot and found I could walk on it, but it was pretty sore.

"Walt, that's a dangerous spot. Why don't you clean your stable out?"

"Stable?" I asked. "What stable?"

Don pointed to the narrow gap under the barn sill

where a gap in the foundation made a crawl-space about five feet wide.

"That's not a stable," I said. "That's where old Fisher kept his chickens. He had to crawl in there on his hands and knees every day to get the eggs."

"Used to be a stable, Walt. I remember when old Fisher kept Clydesdale horses in there."

"He did? Where? When?"

"It's years ago now. But things piled up after a bit and the horses wouldn't go in. So, for a while he used it for steers. Things piled up a bit more and then he used it for veal calves. After that it was pigs. For the last five years or so he just kept chickens."

I looked again at the gap in the foundation.

"Do you actually mean to say . . ."

"Yep. Hard to believe, but down there . . . six feet or so . . . there's a concrete floor."

I remembered the story of King Eurystheus handing Heracles a manure fork and telling him to clean out the Augean stables. Don, being more helpful than the average Greek king, offered to bring over his tractor and loader in the morning and help with the excavations himself. He suggested I ask Freddy for the loan of a tractor and manure-spreader.

At nine o'clock the next morning, I limped up to Freddy's place and found him, or at least his boots, sticking out from underneath his '62 Pontiac, a beer balanced on his chest, poking plug wires up through the manifold. Every so often, Freddy glares at the Pontiac like a peregrine falcon and declares that "this day, that car will run." It never has.

"That spreader . . ." he said, looking at the ground and grabbing his cheek-bones with his thumb and index finger to stimulate his memory. "Seems to me Willy and Dave borrowed that spreader last year. They're out the back, scuffling turnips."

Off we went in Freddy's newer-model Pontiac to see the boys. Now, Willy and Dave have a reputation for getting an enormous amount of work done in record time but whenever I chance upon them, their vehicles are all parked nose to nose in the field, protecting a case of twenty-four. It was in this position that we found them, sadly contemplating a bent rod, which was evidently an important element of turnip-scuffling machinery.

"G'day, fellas," said Freddy. "D'you boys mind the spreader you borrowed off me last year? Where did it get to?"

"Spreader?" said Willy. "Hey, Dave! D'you mind the spreader we borrowed off Uncle Freddy. Where'd it get to?"

"Gee, Willy, didn't that Italian fella up the Town Line borrow it last spring?"

"Yeah, but he lent it to Sparky McEwan, didn't he?"

"Well, most of Sparky's stuff's up at his old man's now."

"But his old man sold out in the spring. Jeez, Uncle Freddy, you did the auction sale, don't you remember?"

"That was my spreader?" said Freddy, looking genuinely shocked. "I only got a hundred bucks for it."

In the meantime Dave had climbed into the driver's seat of Freddy's Pontiac and was examining the dashboard with curiosity.

"Say, this old stove's in pretty good shape, Uncle Freddy. Did you ever think you might sell her?"

Freddy's interest in the spreader vanished. He leaned in the window and started his sales pitch.

"She runs real good, Dave. Now just last summer I put a new set of rods in her."

Dave fired up the motor and put his foot to the floor. There was a roar, and blue smoke spewed out the back as the engine revved up to full throttle. Dave cranked the car into reverse, and for a few moments it sat churning in the same spot, the inside filling up with dust until Dave disappeared from view like the fairy castle in one of those jars you shake up to create a snowstorm. Eventually, the car slid away and began a breakneck lap of the field, still in reverse, setting up a rooster tail of dust and turnip leaves in its wake. At our end of the field, we could still hear Dave's shrill, axe-murderer laugh over the distant roar of the car. As he completed the lap and entered the final turn, Dave tried a forward gear and the car did a lazy swerve towards us, travelled the last hundred yards or so sideways and finally came to rest in a thick clump of choke-cherries in the fence-row. Dust whirled out the windows and Dave gradually reappeared.

"She runs real good, Uncle Freddy," he said, running his finger through the dust on the dashboard. "But you should get her cleaned up a bit! Heeyah, heeyah!"

Freddy wasn't amused. "C'mon, let's go find that spreader."

Freddy had sold the spreader to a man named McGrath. Sure enough, that's where we found it, sagging under a load of barn timbers, a forgotten shipment to a forgotten destination. Freddy studied the timbers for a minute and then decided we would unload them ourselves. Half an hour later, that job was completed and we hooked the spreader to the trailer-hitch on the back of the Pontiac. Just before we left, Freddy thought it would be a good idea to put a load of rails on the spreader for the stretch of fence out behind his house.

By lunch-time we were back at Freddy's. Willy and Dave showed up with their crew and we sat down to a banquet served up by Freddy's long-suffering sister, Maggie. We consumed a quantity of meat, potatoes and turnips, traded hog prices and land values with disbelieving whistles, and observed a moment's silence for the market report. Towards the end of the hour, Dave stood by the open window, picking his teeth with a toothpick.

"Uncle Freddy," he observed. "That spreader of your's got a flat tire."

That set the tone for the afternoon. We got the tire off the spreader by heating the lug bolts with a blowtorch, took it into town and got it plugged at Ron's. A mere two hours later the tire was back on the spreader, the load of rails thrown off behind the house and the spreader hooked up to Freddy's little red Case tractor. For a fleeting moment, it looked as if I might get away after all, but then a shout came from the turnip field.

"We're up to our axles in mud out here," called Willy. "Bring some of them rails and give us a hand."

Freddy turned to me apologetically, to see if I would mind. Of course, I didn't. It turned out to be quite a show. By the end of the afternoon, a crawler had been brought to the scene, escorted by two township road-graders. Another case of twenty-four appeared and this time no fewer than seven different species of vehicle were parked nose-to-nose around it. At 5:23 p.m. the tractor emerged from the mud like an exhausted water-buffalo, to the cheers of men, the roar of machines and the maniacal laughter of Willy and Dave. They all escorted me back to the house, apologizing once again for having kept me so late.

"Never mind," I said. "These things happen." Besides, I pointed out that I could still get a load on back at the farm before supper. Freddy jumped up on the little Case tractor and pushed the starter button.

"RRR . . . RRR . . . rrr . . . rr . . . r . . ."

Freddy turned to me with a sigh. "Y'know, this little tractor never starts unless the sun's on it. I really should give it a charge overnight. Why don't you leave this until tomorrow?"

Why not, indeed. I bade furewell and trudged off down the lane, back to the farm. Maggie waved goodbye from the '62 Pontiac where she was watering geraniums. She always uses Freddy's car as a planter as soon as there's any danger of frost. The last picture of the day remains in my mind; Freddy's feet sticking out from under the car; Maggie absently watering flowers; Willy and Dave sitting under the hollyhocks by the driving shed, smoking roll-yer-owns and reading the racing news.

Back at the farm I discovered that Don had been there and gone ahead without me. A mountainous manure pile greeted me in the barnyard, which I picked my way around to discover my new stable.

There was no sign of King Eurystheus. He'd gone home for the day to milk his cows.

September 20

Don and I were leaning on the pig fence the other day, watching the pigs wander around their pen.

"Say, Walt," said Don. "Those fellas weigh a couple of hundred pounds each. You'll be wanting to send them out next week."

"Mmm? Send who out? Where?"

"These pigs, Walt. They're ready for the freezer."

It gave me a chill, coming on so suddenly like that. I'd never really considered what life would be like without the pigs and I hadn't realized how attached I'd become to them. I tried to explain.

"Don, it's just that . . . well, these aren't just pigs, Don. These are my junior vice-presidents: Abernathy, Greenaway, Pomerantz, Pilkington . . . I recruited them. I brought them into the firm. I gave them objectives to meet—two hundred pounds in the first five months. And they all met the target. Well, maybe it was more like six months. They had a few sick days."

"There you go, Walt. They've outlived their usefulness. What would you do at the firm?"

That was a good question. The answer was . . . probably nothing. That's what they used to say about me at

MacFeeters, Bartlett and Hendrie. They used to say old Wingfield couldn't fire anybody. I hired people every day but I always let Alf Harrison take care of my mistakes. I just never had the stomach for it. Alf used to get upset sometimes and he often complained that his arm was getting tired waving goodbye. I was an ideas person. I thought up new things to do, got new people to join us, whipped everybody into a frenzy when we had a sales campaign, and poor old Alf came along behind me, sweeping up the debris.

Don listened to me for awhile, but before he left he warned me.

"You gotta fire these guys, Walt. They'll eat you out of house and home."

Then it struck me. Maybe I could go into pig-breeding in a really big way. Starting with this stock I could go on to produce the best herd of pigs this township has ever

seen. Anybody looking at these animals could tell at a glance that they were superior stock; long, lean and chunky through the shoulders and hams, with a lovely pink sheen. Any farm would buy the progeny of fine pigs like these.

"You couldn't do that, Walt," said Don, flatly.

"Now, why not?"

"They've been fixed."

November 30

Persuading these two horses that God meant them to work for a living is turning out to be no easier than getting a bond salesman to put in a decent day's work. Where is Alf when I really need him? But at least bond salesmen don't bite and kick. It amazes me how two sleepy old nags can turn into fire-breathing dragons the minute I hitch them to an antique piece of equipment that I have rescued from someone's lawn. To date, they have demolished two single-furrow ploughs, a stone boat, sheared off three mailboxes and kicked a perfectly charming little democrat wagon to kindling.

The day before yesterday they got away from me while I was cultivating the top field and broke for the barn. The cultivator wedged so tightly in the barn door that it took Freddy an hour to cut it free with an acetylene blowtorch. While the horses and I studied one another over the wreckage, Freddy stepped in between us to make a suggestion.

"Walt, why don't you get someone down here to b-b-break this team in properly. Someone who knows what he's doin'. People are startin' to take the S-s-sixth Line into Larkspur just so's they won't meet you and these horses on the road. It's true, Walt. I'll tell you what. I'll send Jimmy down in the morning to give you a hand, but, Walt, don't let him talk you into takin' him into town. He'll go on a toot for sure. He's real frail and he can't take the booze like he used to."

I agreed to this proposal and the next morning Jimmy appeared after chores and watched while I tethered Feedbin and Mortgage to the fence for the harnessing. The girls always stand quietly for this part. It's later on, in ticklish situations, that they start to act up. But the harness has been broken in so many different places now that it all has to be wired together with fence pliers. Jimmy watched this silently until I had finished and then he sighed.

"All right, Walter," he said. "It'll have to do for today. But, if it's all the same to you, we won't drive them through the fashionable part of town."

He noticed Mortgage striking her right front hoof against the fence, gradually splintering the cedar rails until there was a hole big enough for a man to crawl through. This moved Jimmy to poetry:

"If he bites and kicks, you mind him well,
But a harse that strikes is straight from hell."

For practice, Jimmy recommended that we hook the team up to the front bob of the heavy sleighs. This would let them turn or back up without damaging any equipment. He also suggested we work them in the ploughed field I had been cultivating, where the combination of uneven ground and wet snow would make them concentrate on their footing. I took a deep breath of relief. It sure was nice to be working with an expert for once.

Jimmy climbed onto the bale of straw we had tied on the sleigh bob and prepared to start. Now, when I start these horses I just loosen the tension of the lines and give a little chirrup, just like Marshal Dillon giving the schoolmarm a lift into town. Not Jimmy. He whacked the horses over the backside with the lines and yelled "GIDDAP!!"

The horses leapt forward and Jimmy somersaulted backward over the straw bale into the slush. I ran to intercept the runaway team and managed to get my hands on the lines. They were tight as piano wire. I turned to see Jimmy, still holding the lines, rising up out of the icy slush hole like a Polaris submarine, gaunt and terrible in his rage.

"Whoa, you rotten, scum-suckin', yellow-bellied son of a Mohawk . . ."

"WHOOAA!"

Incredibly, the horses stopped and stood trembling, waiting for Jimmy's next command. I don't think they'd ever heard anyone swear in complete sentences before. Jimmy climbed back up on the straw bale, icy water dripping off his chin, his eyes bright and his jaw set. Again he whacked the horses over the backside and yelled "Giddap!" even louder than before. Away they went, off up the lane towards the top field, with me cantering along behind. They plunged into the top field and for a moment all I could see was clods of half-frozen dirt flying through the air. They travelled in a wide arc around the field. It was a scene from the wall of a Roman temple: Pluto descending into the underworld. And then . . . his line snapped.

The horses swerved to the left, Jimmy hauling on his remaining line in a desperate attempt to head them into the fence before they gained the gate and a free downhill run to the barn. It was going to be close. I stood there in the gateway, shouting and waving my arms as the horses bore down on me. All the horse stories I'd ever read assured me that a horse would never trample a man in battle. But there we were, eyeball to eyeball at the gate, and my nerve left me. I jumped aside.

As always, it was a compromise. The horses cleared the gate but the sleigh didn't. One of the iron runners caught the gatepost and stopped dead. Jimmy followed the horses in a graceful trajectory that ended in a clump of thistles. The horses disappeared off down the lane, the loose ends of the harness still flapping in the breeze.

I am concluding this entry from the bar of the Commercial Hotel in Larkspur, where Jimmy and I have been holed up for the last day and a half. I'm wondering how to break the news to Freddy. Still, frail as we are, we're safer in here with the booze than we are out there with the horses.

February 4

I trudged out to the mailbox this morning, through four-foot drifts of snow and an icy wind, for news of the outside world. My reward for the effort was one of those fat window envelopes from the credit-card company, just bristling with bad news. The amount-due box read two thousand five hundred dollars.

I waded back to the house, wheezing and gasping and wondering where all that money had gone. In the summer kitchen, I paused to look again at the bill, and several individual items caught my attention. There was six hundred dollars for feed from the Co-op, including a bag of Hoof'n'Hock Horse Treat. The stuff costs more than granola. Three hundred dollars for hardware for the barn door that blew off its hinges and hit the Hydro line, before it came through the kitchen window. Two hundred and eighty dollars for alcohol for the space-heater in the bathroom. For the first time in years, I felt the cold, sinking feeling of insolvency. I hadn't felt like this since the last time I had bank money in my margin account and the market was on its way down. It seemed worse, in fact, to be starting through all this again, at my age.

I looked up to see the township snow-plough coming down the lane, with Freddy at the controls; Jimmy, Don and The Squire riding shotgun. I thanked them all for ploughing me out, knowing that it would all blow back in within the hour.

"We'll take another pass at it on the way out, Walt," said Freddy.

"We brought you a case of beer," said Jimmy.

I let them all in and they settled around the wood-stove. Still thinking about the credit-card bill, I shuffled around in my sock feet, making toast and coffee, listening to the conversation but not hearing very much. Don's voice brought me back out of my daze.

"Pretty quiet today, Walt. You gettin' cabin fever?"

I explained to him that I was just fretting about bills. They all commiserated, and soon I was telling them the full extent of my troubles. The firm hasn't given me a settlement because the term of our agreement ends on June first, when I'm supposed to decide whether I want to come back or not. But buying the land took most of my savings and the rest has disappeared with all the improvements and purchases I've made this past year. In the meantime, bills keep coming in. Feed, hardware, fuel; bills, bills, bills. It just never seems to stop.

"What income do you have, Walt?" asked Don.

"Income!" I exclaimed. "This is February. What makes money in Persephone Township in February?"

"Fox bounty," said The Squire.

"Well, how much is the fox bounty?"

"Thirty bucks."

I explained that the scope of my problems was a lot larger than thirty bucks, but Freddy persisted.

"You have to kind of m-m-manage the fox bounty," he said. "Now just last week, there's a fella got a fox and he took the right ear to Demeter Township and he got thirty dollars. Then he took the left ear to Pluto Township and he got another thirty dollars. Then he sold the tail to Persephone Township for thirty dollars. That's ninety dollars for a fox."

I wasn't convinced that this would help. I had no intention of shooting at a fox and besides, I hadn't seen one since I came up here. But they kept making suggestions until they were back on familiar topics.

"If you sent those pigs out when I told you," said Don, "you'd be back even by now."

"That orchard," said The Squire, "would have about forty cords of good burnin' wood in it. There's a lot of work but you could get twenty dollars a cord for it."

"Old King would run about seventeen hundred pound," said Jimmy, "Up to Owen Sound they'll give you ten cents a pound."

"For Pete's sake, Jimmy!" I protested. "I can't do that. I couldn't do any of the things you're suggesting."

The Squire shook his head sadly. "If you won't help yourself, Walt, there's nothing we can do."

Then I told them what was in the back of my mind. I told them about the letter from Alf Harrison this week, my old partner at the firm, asking me to come back, even if only for a couple of days a week. The market's been very slow, they're losing clients and they want me to go around and warm up business for them. I could take the train down and they'd pay my hotel bill for whatever nights I stay over. I thought maybe one of the neighbours might help with the chores when I was away.

"Don't do it, Walt," said Freddy. "Gosh, you're working hard enough as it is. It'd ruin your health."

"Freddy's right," Don said, in his solemn way. "You can't put a price on your health." He paused for a moment while we all absorbed the wisdom of this observation. Then he asked, "How much are they offering?"

"The usual," I explained. "A thousand dollars a day plus expenses."

I might as well have said a million. Their eyes widened and they all looked at one another with open mouths. After a moment, The Squire made a suggestion.

"Walt, maybe you could try it for a week or two. We could keep a close eye on you . . . see if you lose any condition."

It isn't exactly what I had in mind but maybe I should try it out for awhile. I'm not ready to give up the farm altogether; it would be too much of a disappointment to my neighbours. They say that watching me this past year has been the most fun they've had since the tax department tried to do an audit on Freddy.

THE SECOND YEAR

ANOTHER NOTE
FROM THE EDITOR

That's pretty much how it went the first year. Soon after his chat with the neighbours, Walt agreed to start back at the firm part time. He bought a computer terminal and set up a trading link with the stock exchange in the summer kitchen. Two days a week now he takes the train to the city where he attends management meetings, gives motivational lectures to the staff and makes pronouncements to the media about the economy.

Things started to improve right away for MacFeeters, Bartlett and Hendrie with Walt back in the chair, doing what he knew best, but back on the farm, Walt was still going through his own private little recession. It would have finished you or me, but Walt didn't quit. He was determined to keep up with this divided life until the farm could pay its way . . . which will not be in his lifetime. But, finances aside, it was a smart move.

The change seemed to give him his old energy back. By the time the snow started to melt, he was writing out a corporate plan for the farm, setting objectives for all the animals again—"the staff" as he calls them. Then, one morning in late March, he pushed another one of his letters through the mail-slot. Just to look at him, you could tell he had regained his confidence and was all set to drive off another cliff.

He saw me through the window and stopped long enough to tell me that his pigs, Pomerantz, Pilkington, Greenaway, Abernathy and the boys, each weighed four hundred pounds and he had decided to appoint them to the board of directors.

And so, the correspondence began again . . .

Dear Ed: March 17

The compensation for working two days a week in the city is the relief that comes with escaping back to the country on the train when business is finished for another week.

With each passing mile, the cares of the office leave me and my shoulders get a little farther from my ears. But I don't get the firm completely out of mind until the train crosses Highway 13 and the hills of Persephone appear on the horizon ahead. The countryside grows more familiar and I start to notice some of the changes that have taken place in the few days since I've been away.

Oscar McKeown must have broken down and paid his taxes this week, because the township snow-blower is finally punching its way up Sharp's Hill to his place, through a ten-foot snow-drift.

The light was fading quickly as the train slowed for the Larkspur station. Standing on the platform was a gaunt old man in a ragged duffle-coat, lime-green pants and a ski toque that said "Parker's Cleaners." As I stepped off the train he started towards me. It was Jimmy.

"G'day, Walt," he said. "I hitched up the team and the sleigh to give you a lift home . . ."

I couldn't believe it. Harnessing those two horses is tricky enough with two people. It would take a lot of nerve for a man in his eighties to try it by himself. But still, it gave me a warm feeling to think what my colleagues back at the firm would say. While they were fighting their way home on the expressway, here was I, skimming along over snowy country lanes in a two-horse open sleigh, sleighbells ringing, spirits singing . . .

"So, did you have any trouble?" I asked.

"Some," said Jimmy. "The bay mare wouldn't come out of the barn. She backed out of the stall all right but she wouldn't come any farther."

"How did you get her out?"

Jimmy chuckled and I presumed he had come out the victor in this dispute.

"I put a good halter on her . . . and I put the harness on the chestnut . . . then I hooked the tugs into the ring on the halter and the chestnut pulled her out like she was on wheels."

It was my turn to laugh.

"You know all these tricks, Jimmy. Now, what would you do if it was a really big horse and it wouldn't leave the barn? What sort of technique would you use then?"

"What you do, Walt," he said, "first you take the halter off, and you make sure you got a good footing. Then you kinda let your shoulders go loose . . . and then you punch him right between the eyes."

"Good heavens, would you really do that?"

It was chilly and we had a long drive ahead, but Jimmy had time for a horse story.

"Oh yeah. Now, there was a fella . . . years ago . . . Orval Ransier. He had a place north of the Pine River. He was a big man and he had a big harse. And that harse quit on him in the stable. He couldn't whip him out and he couldn't drag him out."

I knew this part. "He just quit, right?"

"That's right. So he took the halter off . . . got hisself a good footing . . . and he leaned right into her. Now, you won't believe this, Walt, but that horse ducked. And his fist went right through the wall of the barn . . . and he followed it. When Orval sat up in the snow, that harse was standing right beside him. And the two of them got on just fine after that."

We both laughed and I picked up my suitcase. It was

dark and time we headed for home. I looked over Jimmy's head to the parking lot but saw no sign of the sleigh.

"So, where are the horses?" I asked.

"The bay mare's at McKelvey's."

"Where's the chestnut?"

"After an accident . . . she generally goes once around the concession and then she goes home."

"An accident? Jimmy . . . are you all right?"

"I'm fine. Hard to tell about the car though . . . until they get her out of the ditch."

"You ran someone off the road?"

"Lawyer fella named Darcy Dixon. He tried to pass me over Short's Hill. You know how competitive them harses are."

"So . . . how is he?"

"Mad as hell, as far as I could tell."

Then I noticed the police cruiser waiting behind the station, and Jimmy explained that the young constable had offered to give us a lift back down to the farm. We climbed into the cruiser and drove off down the Seventh Line. At Short's Hill we passed the abandoned sleigh and, a few yards farther on, the Larkspur tow-truck was winching a big, black Cadillac up the side of the ditch onto the road-bed. Dixon was nowhere to be seen.

I must confess I felt awkward about being delivered home by the police. I suppose it's silly really, but I didn't like the idea of a cruiser driving down my lane for all the neighbours to see. I suggested to Jimmy that we drop him off first and I could walk down to the farm from there.

"No, Walter," he said. "Just drop me at the road here. I know this young fella's got business to attend to . . . criminals to catch . . ."

"Oh, I'm sure he doesn't mind. You don't have any criminals to catch tonight, do you, Officer?"

The officer gave a faint smile but made no reply. He swung into Freddy's lane and coasted down the lane to the house, which to my surprise was cloaked in darkness. The hounds jumped out in the headlights of the cruiser. We thanked the officer, got out and groped our way inside the house.

"Where do you suppose Freddy is?" I asked, fumbling for the light. "It's not like him to be out at this hour."

"Oh, I expect he's around somewhere . . ." Jimmy answered.

He stamped the floor with his heel three times. The trapdoor in the middle of the floor rose about eight inches and Freddy's face appeared.

"Is that you Jimmy? J-j-jeez! . . . You scared the d-d-daylights out of us!"

And up they came: Freddy and Maggie, with several assorted cats and dogs. When Freddy saw me, he sighed.

"Walt," he said. "We're glad to see you anytime. But if you want to bring the whole police force with you . . . j-j-just call ahead, will you?"

Just another quiet evening in the country.

April 1

Winter lets go of this land with the reluctance of an old dog giving up a bone.

This morning, I stood on the hill across the road, looking back up the Seventh Concession towards Larkspur, and felt the light drizzle seep into every pore. Pockets of fog lay in the swamp and back along the stream to the barns, where a motley group of steers stood apart from each other, chewing and, every so often, coughing clouds of steam. The horses hung their heads out the barn windows, watching the icicles drip from the eaves into icy pools. The hens sat in a silent row on the pig-feeder, feathers fluffed. Everyone wore the same dazed expression that I remember so well from subway platforms and bus shelters, the unmistakeable sign that the novelty of winter has completely worn off.

Shrugging off the feeling of despondency, I started up, gave a shout to Spike and fell flat on my face in the wet snow. I sat up spluttering and saw that I'd tripped over an orange-tipped stake, the kind surveyors use on road projects . . . or building sites. But what was a surveyor's stake doing in the middle of an empty pasture?

I looked to my left and saw another one. To my right a third. I shuffled around through the snow and uncovered about twenty-five of them over the next ten minutes, all the while wondering what on earth was being planned. If this was a building, it was no ordinary sugar shack.

"G'day, Walt. D'you lose a nickel?"

I looked up and saw The Squire, leaning up against his

fence and watching me with an amused expression.

"Do you know who is putting these stakes in the ground?" I asked.

"Sure. Lawyer fella from the city bought this fifty acres off Calvin Currie just last fall. Everybody knows that, Walt. The stakes are probably from the deed survey."

"He's done more than survey it. He's got a building site marked off right here across the front of the property."

"Yeah, I know. It's gonna look real nice. They sent me a brochure that tells you all about it. Come on over and I'll show it to you."

We went back to The Squire's house and he pulled the brochure out of a drawer. It looked like a menu cover from one of those fern bars on Yorkville Avenue, all done in delicate pastel greens and pinks.

"Persephone Glen Homes," said The Squire, reading from the brochure copy. "A quiet enclave of distinguished residences in a country setting."

"Oh, no," I said. "Condominiums." My heart sank as he read on.

". . . significantly only forty-two homes."

"Forty-two!?" I shouted, frightening one of the cats out from under the wood-stove. "Only forty-two homes! Good heavens, man! And you knew about this?"

"Oh yeah."

"I don't believe it. The man sneaks in, buys up land and puts up forty-two condominiums right beside you . . . and you don't object?"

"What would I object to, Walt?"

"It's good agricultural land."

"Good ag . . . ah, go on, Walt," he scoffed. "A rabbit couldn't live off that field unless he had a job in town."

"Well, all right then, maybe it isn't the best land, but . . . it's a natural area."

The Squire snorted again. "There ain't a fence, or a barn or a drain on the whole fifty acres and you call that natural? It's just waste land now, Walt. Wouldn't it be better for someone to make use of it?"

There was nothing I could say to rouse him to any sort of objection. I decided to strike out for the township offices and gather some information firsthand. I dispensed with the horses and borrowed Don's truck for the trip. This was important.

The local government offices for Persephone Township are located in the hamlet of Hollyhock on the banks of the Boyne River. What draws most of the visitors to Hollyhock is a factory that produces ornamental cement statuary—rabbits, dwarves, deer, that sort of thing. Most people wouldn't notice the renovated schoolhouse at the corner that serves as our township offices.

In the office, I was welcomed by the receptionist and asked to take a chair. The township clerk would see me in a moment. She asked me if I would like to read something in the meantime and gave me a pamphlet on tile drainage. After a few minutes she came back and led me to the clerk's office. He was an immense man with a red splotchy face, a gentle expression of hospitality and a handshake that felt like grabbing the end of a two-by-six board.

"Won't you sit down, Mr. Wingfield?" he said in a deep, soothing baritone voice.

"Thank you. I'd like some information about a development that's being put up on the property across from me."

"Oooohhh yeah," he said in a singsong way that sounded oddly familiar. "What is the lot and concession number, Mr. Wingfield?"

"Part of the East Half Lot Twenty-six, Concession Seven," I said.

He flipped slowly through a large binder.

"Yeah. We give a permit to a Mr. Darcy Dixon of Toronto on or above the tenth day of February of this year."

"Well," I said firmly, "I object to it and I want to know why I wasn't informed."

The clerk raised his eyebrows and studied me more carefully. Then he said something I didn't understand.

"You reside on the Adjasson property, do you?"

"The what?"

"Do you reside on the Adjasson property?"

"Adj . . . I believe it was the old Fisher place. Could you spell that for me?"

"A-D-J-A-C-E-N-T."

"Oh . . . oh, yes. Adjasson. Right across the road, in fact. On the West Half of Lot Twenty-six."

The clerk closed the book and said with grave finality, "Then you was circulated."

"No, I don't believe I was. That's why I'm here."

A wrinkle appeared over his left eyebrow. "If you wasn't circulated then you gotta give us notification."

"That's what I'm doing right now."

A wrinkle and a dent appeared over his right eyebrow. "Then you hafta file an appeal."

"I'd like to do that."

A long line appeared over the dents and wrinkles. "Then you gotta fill out an appeal form."

"Could I have one please?"

He shook his head, gave a large asthmatic sigh through his nostrils, and I prepared for the worst. "Yeah," he said and produced a form from the top drawer of his desk. He licked a pencil, squinted at the page and began asking questions.

"All right, Mr. Wingfield. You live on the West Half of Lot Twenty-six. Does the subject lands lie within six hundred feet of the repellent? . . . Uh-huh. They do." He ticked off a box and continued reading.

"Are yous a full-time resident of the township?"

"Yes," I said, too quickly. He looked at me sceptically,

smiled a conspiratorial smile and checked another box. Then he turned the page over and asked:

"Have you had rabies on the property in the past ten years?"

"What?"

"Oh"—he paused and scratched his head sheepishly—"that's another application."

He got me to sign my name at the bottom of the form and then we embarked on the question of when my appeal would be heard.

"The Planning Committee hears the appeals," he said. "They meet on the second Tuesday of the month," I looked at my watch.

"That was just yesterday. He'll have half the houses up by the next meeting."

"Yep," said the clerk, "it's the buildin' season. He'll wanna get into the ground next week."

"But what about my appeal?"

"Well, generally it's the Committee that turns the appeals down. But you could come to township council meetin' next Tuesday week and they'd do it for you then."

This didn't sound very encouraging but I pressed on. "I want to make my views known and get this decision reconsidered. This permit is just opening the door to anyone who wants to sell his farm for condominiums."

"I can see how you feel."

"Isn't there something that can be done before it's too late?"

The clerk leaned back in his creaky chair and took off his glasses.

"Well, you know, Mr. Wingfield," he said, "what you might do is go on over and have a chat with Mr. Dixon and see if you can't work something out between the two of yous. You just never know, and he seemed like a nice enough fella to me. I'm sure he'd listen to reason."

Condominium developers can hear a hundred-dollar bill drop on a thick carpet but they cannot hear reason.

"I'm afraid the time has passed for that," I said. "I would like to make a presentation to council."

"You want to have your day in court, do you? I understand. You come on over here on the fifteenth. Council starts at eight o'clock sharp."

I rose, shook hands solemnly with him and left. On the way home in Don's truck I began mentally constructing the case I will present in two weeks.

April 8

When I left the clerk's office it was raining hard and it kept raining for the rest of the week, bringing the stream at the farm to its banks. Opening Day for the trout season is only a few weeks away and I sniff the air, knowing that the fish are already on their way upstream.

But, if I were a trout in this township, I would want more than the law on my side. I was puttering at the workbench one day this week when Freddy turned up at the basement door, holding a plastic bag.

"Got a present for you," he said, stepping inside quickly. "Mind if I come in?"

I looked in the bag. It contained a big, fat, rainbow trout about two feet long.

"For Pete's sake, Freddy," I exclaimed. "If they catch you with one of these things they'll take your farm away!"

"Don't w-w-worry about it, Walt. There's no problem. We have native fishing rights up here."

"Uh-huh. So, how did you catch it . . . with a spear?"

Freddy looked shocked. "Good gollies, no. The fish are kinda preoccupied this time of the year. The McKee boy just kicked him out of the stream with his rubber boots."

When Freddy left, I closed all the curtains and stashed the body in the freezer compartment of the fridge. It seemed like the first place the authorities would look but I didn't really have much choice. I laid him out with a couple of bags of corn niblets over him but the tail still stuck up at the side. I put an oven mitt over it. The fish would have to stay there for at least a month before it was legal even to look at it.

Then there was a knock at the door and panic seized me. I slammed the freezer door shut, opened a window and fanned the air with a magazine to dispel the fish odour. I opened the door a few inches. It was The Squire.

"Can I see your fish?" he said, shouldering his way in.

"How did you know I had a fish?" I asked, scanning the road for cars. The Squire went straight to the fridge and opened the door.

"Golly, that one's bigger than mine. Bigger than Don's too. Say, what's the oven mitt doing in there?"

It gradually dawned on me that Opening Day in Persephone Township is the day they all open their freezers and start to eat the fish they've been catching over the past two months.

With all the excitement of seeing a fresh fish so early in the year I couldn't resist the urge to practise a few casts with the fly-rod in the stream down by the road—without a fly, of course. Just feeling the spring of a good graphite rod and the tug of water on the line is all you need to make you think of daffodils and baltimore orioles. It really is true that a man cannot fly-cast and worry at the same time.

My roll-cast and side-cast were both in surprisingly good shape after a six-month absence from the stream. I took a good footing and leaned into a double haul to see if I could generate something over my usual thirty feet.

"Hey there!" called a stern voice up on the road above me. It was the young constable from Larkspur, standing beside his car. I waded out of the water to the bank and waved back.

"I know the season isn't open, officer," I said. "I'm just practising my casting with this fly-rod I got for Christmas."

"You don't practise fishing. Either you're fishing or you're not fishing."

I explained patiently that I certainly was not fishing because I was not using a fly. I pulled up the line and showed him the end completely devoid of fly to make the point crystal clear.

"So you lost it."

While I was sitting in the back of the cruiser, the officer plugged into his national databank for poachers and I amused myself by looking out the window. A group of angelic twelve-year-old boys from up the road climbed down the bank in their rubber boots and headed upstream, little plastic bags sticking out of the pockets of their ski jackets. I was about to say something to the officer, but I let it go.

After all, these are just the recurring signs of spring.

April 14

Doctors carry beepers to tell them when they're wanted in maternity. What is a farmer supposed to carry at this time of the year? My cows are calving, my sheep are lambing and I suppose my goats have got to be kidding. In the middle of all this, one of the steers conked out and was dragged away by Oscar Berry's Dead Stock Removal Service. Our sanitary measures are beyond reproach, we use the latest medicated feed, the penicillin syringe is never dry . . . but the casualty levels still remain unacceptably high.

As Freddy says, the Lord giveth and Oscar Berry taketh away.

I put an extension phone in the barn because I spend so much time down here. It hangs right beside the window in the feed-room and there's a sign on the window saying "COWS—In emergency, break glass, use phone."

The latest head-count is twelve lambs, three calves, a litter of nine pigs from Porkchop, the brood sow, and an unknown number of little bunny-rabbits from my New Zealand Red rabbits, Xerox and Gestetner.

But the big surprise was Mortgage, who has been dragging herself around as if she'd eaten a thirty-six-inch pizza and a case of Diet Coke all by herself. She's always had a great hay-belly but this time she was really bloated up and I got concerned enough to call in the horse experts, Freddy and Jimmy.

"Worms" was the verdict, so off I went to the Co-op for supplies. I gave her a great dose yesterday afternoon and this morning came down in the drizzling rain to find her in her box stall, looking very much relieved, with a little filly standing at her side. My mother used to say that nothing induced labour like a dose of castor oil. The horse experts reappeared and, forgetting their diagnosis of the day before, warned me of the dangerous effects of horse-wormer on a pregnant mare.

But all is well. The vet popped out to make sure they were both all right. He gave the foal a shot, checked to see the mare was milking properly, gave me two aspirins and told me to call him in the morning.

I suppose I'm embarrassed that Mortgage caught me by surprise like that, but then again, I won't have to go to pre-natal classes with her. Just imagine trying to get a horse to learn the Lamaze technique. You don't think about these things until you have to.

Freddy and I sat in the mow of the barn this afternoon, listening to the rain drum on the roof and waiting for the last sheep to bring forth her increase. While we were sitting there a large drop of water hit me on the head and we both looked up.

"Old Fisher," said Freddy, "used to shoot the odd pigeon in here. It's just a small leak, Walt."

"Yes, but it's dripping right where I do my best thinking."

"Do you want to plug her up right now while we've got a minute?"

I didn't think we should be climbing around on a tin roof in the rain. Besides, I didn't have a ladder that would reach that high.

"No, but you got a p-p-pulley rope on a track goin' right under that hole," observed Freddy, studying the barn ceiling. "You could winch me up there on the pulley and I'll put a plug of tar in her. Won't take a minute."

So, we set to work, fashioning a chair-lift out of nylon rope and a milk stool for Freddy to sit in. I started to haul on the rope. It was hard work, but Freddy rose a few feet in the air.

"Ah, Walt?" said Freddy. "Just in case we get into trouble, why don't we put a few b-b-bales of hay around here to give me something soft to land on?"

I let him back down and we prepared a comfortable landing area. I had my doubts about the safety of all this but Freddy reassured me.

"Safe as a church, Walt. Here we go."

I hauled on the rope and let it drop in coils at my feet as Freddy rose in the air. Higher and higher he went till he was dangling twenty feet up, at the second purlin timber, right where the roof was leaking.

"Pretty slick, Walt. I can reach her now."

By one of those funny coincidences that make farm life so interesting, two things happened at that moment. Jimmy appeared in the door of the hay mow and the phone started to ring downstairs in the feed-room.

"Jimmy," I said, "could you hold this rope for me? I'll get that phone."

Jimmy took the rope in both hands, bent his knees and braced himself.

"I got 'er, Walter. You get the phone."

I stepped away, remembering that while Freddy weighed about one-eighty, Jimmy was probably something under a hundred and ten. Jimmy lifted off the ground and sailed up, towards the ceiling. The coils of rope at my feet disappeared in an upward spiral and Freddy came down, crashed through the floor and into the stable below. For a moment, everything stood still. Then the empty chair-lift came back up through the hole in the floor. That meant Jimmy was on his way down. I half caught him and we rolled into the straw landing-pad together. Jimmy let go of the rope. I should have realized instantly what would happen next but I didn't. The chair dropped back down and bounced off my shoulder.

By this time, the phone had stopped ringing. Jimmy and I picked each other up, and Freddy appeared at the top of the feed-room stairs.

"Don't w-w-worry about the phone, Walt," he said. "If it was important, they'll call back."

While I continue to fret about the health of my animals it appears that farmers are far more likely to wipe themselves out before any appreciable dent is made in livestock populations.

By the way, if you need a small bunny-rabbit, or two or three . . . just give me a call.

April 15

I felt a little badly last month when my two geese, Colonel Belknap and General Longstreet, got the chop. I had vague plans to keep them through the winter and try to raise some goslings this spring. But I couldn't tell a daddy goose from a mommy goose for all the pâté in France.

Imagine my surprise when Maggie bought both of them from me for a dollar a pound. That came to twenty-eight dollars—the largest single entry for the month of March. And do you know what they eat?

Grass.

The outlay per gosling was five dollars. Starter feed was two dollars. Summer pasture goes for about ten cents an acre in this economy. Labour costs involved in feeding, killing, plucking and cleaning, and running around trying to sell them are all dismissed as negligible because I haven't got anything better to do anyway. Total expenses: seven dollars and ten cents per goose. Compare this to an average return of fourteen dollars per goose and I think you can see the magic of multiplication working in my favour.

This is very exciting. The upside is nothing short of breath-taking. Today, I created a new subsidiary, Wingfield Pâté Limitée, and went off to Larkspur to purchase supplies.

The General Store in Larkspur is run by a man named McKelvey, who appears to be about the biggest employer in the township. He owns the store, the feed and hardware business out the back, a building supply across the road and five hundred acres along the Pine River, with several hog barns, feedlots and turkey sheds. It's a big operation.

Actually, I prefer to deal with his assistants because they are more friendly. But this morning, when I rode into town, he was standing on the verandah of the store, having just loaded several bags of groceries into a woman's car.

"Goodbye, Mrs. Lynch," he said, pleasantly enough, until the car pulled away. Then he added ". . . and pay your bill sometime!"

He turned back to me and spoke as if I'd been following him around all morning. He has a whiny voice that turns up at the end of each phrase, unlike any other voice I have heard in the township.

"I'll be lucky to get paid for those groceries in six months," he complained, "but she still makes me carry them to the car. She wants me to drop everything the minute she comes into the store, chase around, get stuff off the shelves. Do I have time for that? No. I got a business to run. So what can I do for you?"

"I won't keep you a minute, Mr. McKelvey. I need some starter feed for goslings. Do you have any?"

"Where did you get the goslings?" he asked sharply.

"Ah . . . well, actually I haven't got them yet. I was going to drive down to the Waterloo sales barns and pick some up on Thursday."

"What do you pay for them?"

"Last year they were five dollars."

"Each?" The sound of his voice was beginning to grate on my nerves. "I can get 'em for you a lot cheaper than that!"

"You can?"

"I just got a hundred in this week."

"Well, I only need fifty."

"A dollar each if you take the whole bunch."

I stopped. A dollar each was a good price. "What about the starter pellets?"

"Ten bucks a bag and you'll need ten bags of it."

"Ten bucks? Last year it was five."

"Grain's gone up. I don't run a charity. Do you want the geese or not?"

"Where did they come from?"

"Hatchery away up north." He was being evasive. "They're good birds. They go real fast this time of the year. You want 'em or not?"

"All right . . . sure. Can you deliver them?"

"That's extra."

I told him not to bother, knowing I could get Don to help me. As it turned out, Don wasn't as impressed with the deal as I was. I found him in the mow of his barn, grinding corn, and when I told him what I had just done he turned off the machine and stared at me.

"You bought a hundred geese from Dry Cry?"

"Dry Cry? Why do you call him that, Don?"

"It's his voice, Walt. He sounds like he's cryin' but there's no tears. Did you look at these geese?"

"Ah . . . no I didn't. But they're all the same . . . aren't they? I mean, a goose is a goose . . . isn't it?"

Don was incredulous.

"You bought a hundred geese from Dry Cry and didn't even look at them? I'll tell you a story about that man, Walt. One time he went shares with his brother on five hundred turkeys. But he's so cheap he figured he could save a lot of money if he didn't put the medication and the supplements in the feed like you're supposed to. After a couple of months, half the turkeys were walkin' around on their elbows, all crippled up, so Dry Cry crated up the healthy ones and sold them all down at Waterloo. The next time his brother's in the turkey shed he looks at all these crippled turkeys and says, 'Those turkeys aren't doin' so good.' And Dry Cry says, 'Never mind, those are the ones that lived.'

"And that was his own brother, Walt. Let's go have a look at those geese."

As it turned out, they passed inspection. Dry Cry had them all packed up in those flat cardboard poultry cases with the air-holes in them. But Don unpacked each box and checked them over carefully.

"They look healthy enough," he said, sitting back on his heels. "A little dark . . . What kind are they?"

"They're French," said Dry Cry.

"French?" I said. "That's nice. Did you hear that, Don? French geese."

"Uh-huh," said Don in his solemn way. "They look a little dark to me."

So, we took them all home and Wingfield Pâté Limitée is in business with French geese. I've got them in the feed-room now. They should be ready to go out on the grass in a month. Spike has agreed to be development vice-president of the new company. He's aggressive, self-starting . . . and the only member of the staff who doesn't eat starter pellets.

April 18

On Tuesday night I drove over to council to make my presentation, as planned. The meeting began at eight o'clock, just like the clerk said, but he neglected to tell me that petitions are not heard until the rest of the agenda is completed. I sat and listened as they waded through twenty-two items.

One of the vigilant correspondents was there, from the *Free Press and Economist.* But we heard nothing from him the whole evening except for the sound of his head hitting the desk.

The reeve sat at the middle of the council table, wearing his chain of office with the township crest on it. On his right, in plain clothes, was the deputy-reeve, and on his left, the other two councillors. At a separate table sat my friend, the clerk, who prompted the reeve through the agenda. It all looked like a meeting of the Soviet presidium. None of these people was under sixty-five, and the one on the end looked like a contemporary of Wilfrid Laurier.

"Your worship," said the clerk, "the first item of business we have here is a letter from Demeter Township saying that they don't want to contribute to the Larkspur library agreement anymore."

"What are they whinin' about now?" asked the reeve.

"Seems they've checked over the records and they found that no one from Demeter used the library in the last two years. They say it ain't worth it and they want out."

The councillors looked at each other meaningfully, and the deputy-reeve said, "They ain't had no fire up there this year either, but they ain't askin' to get out of the fire agreement."

"Is it the wish of council," said the clerk, "that I write 'em back while they can still read and tell 'em to go to hell?"

The motion was carried unanimously. In this fashion, council disposed of an application for a trailer-park permit, paid nine sheep-damage claims and approved a permit for a dog-obedience school. They endorsed a circular resolution from a distant municipality calling for nuclear disarmament and then settled down for the road superintendent's report. At about half-past ten it was time for petitions. The clerk introduced me, and they all got up to shake hands with me, which struck me as very hospitable. The reeve invited me to speak.

"Mr. Wingfield," he said, "we sure do appreciate you coming out and takin' an interest in council. As you can see, we run an open meeting and anyone with a complaint can come in here and speak his mind, if he's got one."

"Well," I said. "I appreciate the opportunity to be here. I have a problem with a land severance and building permit you approved across from my property . . ."

The clerk interrupted to explain where my farm is located.

"Denton," he said, addressing the reeve, "this is the old Fisher place at the corner of the Twenty-fifth and the Seventh. Down in the valley there . . ."

"Oh, gollies, yes," said the reeve, nodding, "I know the property, Harold. The Fishers is cousins of my wife's family, and Harriet spent the summer over there the year before we were married, when her dad was burned out. Do you mind that, Ernie?"

Ernie was the deputy-reeve, a red-faced man of an excitable nature. The reeve's apparently innocent observation brought him to the edge of his chair as if a challenge had been issued.

"I took hay off the back fields down there with my dad

ten years before that," he announced, "when the Fishers still lived at the home farm on the Sixth."

Wilfrid Laurier leaned forward from the other side of the reeve and hissed, "My grandfather put the first plough in them fields and held the original deed. It was him sold it to the Fishers."

There was a silence and the reeve looked back at me, inviting me to continue. I was somewhat puzzled by this exchange, but I carried on.

"The property I am concerned about is, in fact, *across* the road . . . the East Half of Lot Twenty-six."

"That would be the back of Calvin Currie's place, Denton," said the clerk, helpfully.

"Oooohh, yesss," said the reeve. "God, that's a stony field. Just a pasture now, but there was a time when it put up sixty bushels to the acre. Used to be a barn on that place. Do you mind that barn, Ernie?"

"Do I?" roared Ernie. "My dad built that barn. It was the first bank barn in the north end of the township. Damn near broke him but he built her. That's a long time ago."

Mr. Laurier leaned forward again. "My great-grandfather," he said in a voice barely audible, "was the first white man to set foot on the Currie farm. He did the original survey the year Princess Victoria took to the throne."

This was starting to get away from me.

"Excuse me," I said, waving one hand, "I would like to appeal a decision you have made to sever fifty acres off that farm and grant a building permit to Darcy Dixon for the construction of forty-two condominiums."

"Harold, did you circulate Mr. Wingfield?" asked the reeve.

"Yes, your worship, the said application was forwarded on or above the thirteenth of February, but the said application failed to arrive. He never seen it."

"You got a mailbox, Mr. Wingfield? Or do you pick it up at the store?"

"I had a mailbox but it disappeared on or above the thirteenth of February," I said, matching the clerk's turn of phrase as diplomatically as I could, "courtesy of the township snow-plough."

"That happens," said the reeve. "I expect it'll turn up when the snow melts and then we'll put her back up for you."

"I appreciate that very much, but what about my appeal?"

"Well, sir, it's too bad you didn't get circulated and no one feels worse about that than I do. I can see it weren't in your power to get your objection heard before the appeal period expired, but the rules is the rules and I'd be takin' the law into my own hands if I told you any different."

"The appeal period has expired?" I said. "When was that?"

"Today at twelve o'clock. Now, I'll tell you what we can do for you, Mr. Wingfield. Harold, here, will get the road superintendent out to your place and they'll fish around in that big drift till they find your mailbox and get her set up again. Now, you'll do that for him, won't you, Harold?"

"Oh yes, Mr. Reeve. We'll do that," said the clerk.

I glared over at the clerk's desk, but he was calmly drawing a heavy line through my name on the agenda. I listened to the reeve's speech of thanks for my appearance, shook hands with everyone and left.

I drove back to Freddy's, my sense of grievance growing with every washboard I drove over. In Freddy's kitchen, Maggie had the gas furnace turned way up, which didn't help. Even the cats had moved into the summer kitchen to cool off.

"If they approve this," I asked Freddy, "what next? Where will they stop?"

"Lot of taxes will be comin' outa that place, Walt. You gotta think of that. It's gettin' late. You want a bit of lunch?"

"Lunch? It's past midnight."

Maggie produced crackers, cheese, cold cuts, pickles, apple pie, maple syrup and a pot of tea, and called us to the table.

I pulled out a chair and said, "Dammit, Freddy . . . the only way to get this thing under control is to run for council myself."

I had expected Freddy to be surprised, but I wasn't prepared for the look of woe that contorted his face.

"D-d-don't do it, Walt," he warned. "You'll learn to hate yourself. You know what it means, takin' a job like that? Hand out dog licences . . . keep the roads fixed up . . . and have every lunatic in the township callin' you to get their lane ploughed out."

"There's a principle at stake here," I argued. "I'm going to put my name up for the municipals next September."

"Walter . . . people run for council when they've run out of stupid things to do on their own place . . . and you got a long way to go there yet. You haven't even scratched the surface."

"Freddy," I said patiently, "it's easy to be cynical. But you and I know that if you want good government you have to get involved, and where better than here?"

"After all, government at the township level is the very touchstone of democracy. It's what built this country and produced its great leaders, people like . . ."

Names escaped me for the moment. But Freddy knew what I meant. I predicted that in a year's time the people of this great township will probably come to think of me in much the same way as the people of Illinois saw Abraham Lincoln, or the way the people of Rome saw Cincinnatus—one hand on the plough, the other on the tiller of the ship of state.

Freddy was impressed. "By golly, we got ourselves a public figure here, Maggie. Gosh, Walt, that's powerful stuff . . . speakin' of which, let's have a toast to the candidate. What about that special bottle we got at Christmas, Maggie?"

Maggie opened one of the high cupboard doors and looked at a row of liquor bottles.

"Which is the special one, Freddy?" she asked.

Freddy poured us both a glass and Maggie offered to toast the occasion with a mug of hot Horlick's Malt. As we raised our glasses Freddy paused and said, "I gotta warn you, Walt. Elections around here are a little different than what you may be used to back home. If you're determined to go ahead with this, maybe me and the boys should give you a hand."

"Will you be my campaign manager?" I asked.

"Now, that would be a good idea. Here's to you, Walt."

So, there you have it. I am a candidate for the municipals in October and I've already done some work on my speech to the all-candidates' meetings.

"My friends . . . for we are all friends here . . . Our challenge will be to face, head on, the promise of our future . . . without losing sight of the traditions of our heritage . . .

Keeping one eye on the rich potential of our township . . . but, on the other hand, resisting the urge to creep before we walk . . ."

Well, it sounded better when I gave it to the steers this morning. And don't laugh. Freddy says he can get them on the voters' list.

June 12

This used to be my favourite view. Looking out the hay-mow door, over the manure pile, I still have a commanding vista of the Seventh Concession and the Pine

River Valley. But last week, bulldozers and back-hoes moved on to Darcy Dixon's pasture and began ripping it apart. What used to be an attractive natural setting of limestone rock and cedar trees is now one vast, gaping wound. It would take me and the horses a month to make it look like that. A huge billboard at the fence-line, in the same hideous pastels of the brochure, announces "Persephone Glen Homes—Elegance in Harmony with Nature—from $250,000."

Dixon told me he was going to plant a wind-break, so his buyers wouldn't have to look at my place. The next day a truck arrived carrying seventy-five Siberian elms twenty feet tall. By the end of the afternoon he had created an instant forest.

The neighbours think it's just great. "Good for the tax base," they say or, "You can't stop progress." I seem to be the only person on the concession who doesn't think it's a good idea. I tried to appeal to their sense of history by pointing out that Calvin Currie's farm has been in his family's name for a hundred and fifty years. He has a Century Farm sign at his gate.

I asked: "What does a Century Farm sign mean to you people?"

The answer was: "A hundred years without a single decent offer for your land."

It doesn't do to dwell on these things. I have other things to worry about, like my geese, for example. They just started growing their adult feathers and I had a good look at them on Sunday. They're not French at all—there's nothing French about them. They're Canada geese . . . all one hundred of them.

I had a visit from a wildlife officer of the Ministry of Natural Resources yesterday. He tells me it's illegal to feed Canada geese, and he gave me a week to release them back to the wild. That's all very well for him to say. A hundred geese haven't imprinted on his overalls.

I was right about one thing. They eat grass all right. There isn't a blade of grass left around the barn, and the only thing that keeps them away from the house is gunfire. They careen around the place like marauding riff-raff, terrorizing everyone.

My old rule for times like this is to stay busy as much as possible. Having declared my candidacy in public I decided to gear up the campaign committee in the clinch-the-deal atmosphere of the Little Red Hen Restaurant in Larkspur. I phoned Freddy late Monday night to arrange a power breakfast for the key strategists.

The rule at the farm is, the animals eat before you do, which may be one reason that breakfast meetings have never caught on in the country. We all staggered into the Little Red Hen the next morning, and I realized what time Don must have got up to milk fifty cows and get there by eight o'clock.

"Is this gonna happen a lot in this campaign?" asked Don, looking at me through bleary, red eyes.

"Breakfast meetings are important," I said. "They communicate a feeling of commitment and show people we're up early and working hard. Now, have you got any suggestions about how I conduct myself during the campaign . . . where I should go, what I should say?"

"You gotta stay outa sight until the vote," said Don.

I laughed politely and continued. "I realize that it's going to be a tough battle and all that, but this is the challenge of a campaign . . . the cut-and-thrust of debate, meeting the people face to face, main-streeting, door-knocking . . . do you think maybe I should go to the senior citizens' home?"

They looked at each other.

"I never thought of that," said Don. "We could get you

a room there for the month with my dad. Nobody would know you were there."

"Now hold on a minute," I protested. "I can't hide from the people. A peekaboo campaign is not my style. We're going to face this thing head on and deal with the issues as——"

"What Don is saying," interrupted Freddy, "is that people don't know you as well as we do. Three weeks isn't much time to convince them to go votin' for you. You'd be a lot b-b-better off if we put some signs up and you just lay low down at the farm . . . Hey, Donna? Could we have coffee over here?"

"I'm as good as the next man. I pay my taxes. Is there something wrong with me?"

"You ain't been hit by lightning," said The Squire.

"Lightning?"

"Now you take the fella who topped the polls the last three votes. He was hit by lightning on his barn roof about ten years ago. Never was the same after that. Couldn't farm and he couldn't do anything else. So we said, why not put him on council? Perfect for the job. That lightning was the making of him as a politician."

"I see," I said. "He avoids controversy, does he?"

"He avoids breathin' when he can."

Donna brought four cups of coffee to the table.

"There you go, Walt," said Freddy, passing me a cup. "If you don't want sugar, don't stir. Now, you sure you don't want to go into the nursing home? They got a new pool table, and shuffle-board . . ."

"No," I said flatly. "The next item on the agenda is fund-raising. Have any of you ever done any fund-raising before . . . for something like this?"

"Oh sure," said The Squire. "We got three hundred dollars once for the furnace in the church."

"Great. When was that?"

"Nineteen fifty-four."

I pointed out that with printing and advertising expenses the campaign costs could approach a thousand dollars. Just then, the lights and the radio went off and the fan over the deep-fryer whirred to a halt.

"That'll be Willy and Dave," said Freddy. "They're takin' a m-m-maple tree down outside Dry Cry's."

"Looks like it's down now," said Don. "We better get out there and give them a hand."

"Yep," agreed The Squire. "If they try doing home repairs on them wires we'll have another couple of candidates for office."

We went outside. It was a warm June morning and across the highway in front of the General Store a huge maple tree lay in a splash of green. Willy and Dave stood sadly contemplating the exposed end of a Hydro wire, snapping and guttering on the ground. On its way down, the tree had caught on the cement porch of the store and pinned a table of fresh produce to the wall. This appeared to be the only damage to the store, but Dry Cry was in a temper, threatening to sue for willful damage and interruption of business. When the Hydro truck arrived, the servicemen isolated the pole, reconnected the wires and handed Willy and Dave a bill for five hundred dollars.

"Five hundred dollars?" said Willy. "Hoooooeeeeeey!"

A sum like that can take your mind right off an election campaign.

"Hate to see a bunch of people get up so early and still be this far behind," said The Squire sadly. "How are you at fund-raising, Walt?"

Dry Cry was only paying Willy and Dave fifty dollars to take down the tree in the first place. That left us four hundred and fifty to raise from other sources. We set off up the street to find someone who would either buy the wood or pay us to take down another tree. Mrs. Cole's eaves-troughing was suffering from the attention of a willow tree, and the rectory had a patch of shingles missing where a maple branch was scraping the garage roof, but our reputation had preceded us. There were no takers. However, the minister did offer to buy three cords of firewood, cut and stacked alongside his garage, for a hundred dollars. That left three hundred and fifty dollars still to raise and the morning was already half gone.

We spent the next two hours in front of Dry Cry's hacking away at the maple tree and loading it into Don's pick-up. The racket from two man-killing chain-saws brought all conversation to a halt and we were each left alone with our fund-raising plans for the afternoon. Back at Freddy's for lunch, Maggie received the news in something less than stoic silence.

"You take on a job for half what anyone else would charge and you come home owing a month's wages. We'd be farther ahead if you sat in there all day, watching television."

A Pyrex bowl of turnips hit the table with some force. She returned to the kitchen, and Freddy leaned over the table to me.

"Don't worry about Maggie, Walt. She's just a bit upset with the boys because they might have been hurt with that live wire. She worries about them . . ."

From the kitchen Maggie shouted over the running taps: "For five hundred dollars I'd put them both in a hot bath with a toaster oven."

We finished the meal in silence and slunk out to the summer kitchen to plan strategy for the afternoon. We delivered the wood to the minister, piled it along the garage and returned to the store for a Coke. Sitting on the verandah, we listened to Dry Cry's attempt to extract damages from Willy and Dave for the bent table.

"I'm willing to forget the interruption of business, but look what you done to my table!" he whined.

"Ah, go on, Dry Cry," said Don. "There ain't a scratch on it."

Don was right. It suddenly struck me how sturdy a table it was to have carried the weight of a tree with so little damage. I peeked under the linoleum and ran a fingernail over a patch of exposed wood.

"I could use a table like this in the barn," I said to Dry Cry. He screwed up his face and I prepared for another assault on my ears.

"It'd cost me fifty bucks to make a new one."

"If I gave you thirty-five, would you take it?"

"Forty," he said, sticking his nose in my face.

"Don't give in to him, Walt," said The Squire. "He's so narrow he could walk through the strings of a harp without strikin' a note."

"Done," I said, and handed him two twenties.

Dry Cry looked at me suspiciously for a moment and then reached out and took the bills.

In Freddy's yard, we unloaded the table from the truck and I borrowed Don's penknife to score the old linoleum and turn it back. The table top was one solid pine board an inch and a half thick and thirty inches across.

"Gentlemen," I announced, "I believe we just broke even. With a little sandpaper and a coat of urethane, this table is worth seven hundred dollars."

"Who would pay seven hundred dollars for this?" asked The Squire.

"Darcy Dixon, QC."

And he did. Our campaign kitty now has three hundred and ten dollars in it.

July 12

I am learning, with the great statesmen of the world, that the price of peace is eternal vigilance, especially when you're in the poultry business. Late last night, just as I was settling into the feathers for the night, I heard the piercing scream of a chicken from down at the barn.

You have to hear that sound yourself to understand why

it brings you out of bed at a dead run and sends you flailing down the lane in pyjamas and slippers. As the barn loomed up before me, I could hear squawks, flutters and thuds coming from the hen pen. I flung open the door and switched on the lights. There was a scurrying along the wall, and a small dark shape vanished through a crack in the boards.

In the hen pen, all was confusion. Four hens lay on the floor, feathers fluffed out and breathing their last. The survivors huddled together on the roost, clucking nervously and scolding me: "Book, book, book . . . you're the sheriff, can't you do something about this?"

I did my best to quiet the ladies and bent down to pick up the casualties. Boots appeared in the doorway in front of me and I looked up with a start. It was Don, carrying a twelve-gauge shotgun.

"Heard the noise," he said. "How many did he get?"

"These four," I said, pointing to the bodies lying on the straw. "What do you mean, 'he'?"

Don turned one of the hens over with the toe of his boot and pointed under the wing with the gun barrel.

"See that?" he said in a low voice. "It's tough enough to keep a hen layin' every day without a hole in it like that. That's the work of a weasel. They come in when it's dark and climb up on the roosts. They move so quietly that the hens don't even know they're there. Then they pick one out and grab it under the wing, just here . . ."

Don poked me under the arm and I jumped about six inches off the ground. He sat down on a cement block and cradled the gun in his arms.

"He'll be back before long. When he does . . . we'll be here."

"We will? I mean . . . how do you know he'll be back?"

"Once he's got the taste of blood, there's only one way to stop him."

This was all starting to sound like an episode of "Gunsmoke."

"Say, Don, you won't fire that thing without giving me a little warning, will you?"

"Turn out the light, Walt . . . and make yourself comfortable. We may be here for awhile."

I turned out the light and sat down in the straw, beside Don, facing the chickens. The hens were roosting quietly now, their little chicken pulses already back to normal despite the recent visit of a serial murderer.

"Don?" I said tentatively.

"Yeah?"

"Is it all right to talk?"

"I suppose so," he said. "But I'm not very conversational."

"How come?"

"I had a visit from Darcy Dixon today."

"You did? What did he want?"

"He told me he doesn't want me spreadin' any more manure on the front fields. Says it isn't good for business."

"What?" I exclaimed, a surge of adrenalin rushing through me. "What did you say to him?"

"Nothing," said Don.

"He can't tell you how to farm, Don."

There was a pause, then Don said quietly, "Maybe you were right, Walt. That Dixon fella's gettin' to be a real pest." We lapsed into silence again.

Time does not pass quickly in the dark, especially when you're fighting sleep. But the important thing in a stakeout is to stay alert.

My eyelids started to droop and I pinched myself awake. I thought about Darcy Dixon and his condominiums. That gave me a few minutes of wakefulness but soon I was drifting again.

Then I remembered the weasel and jerked upright. I had to stay awake. I tried to imagine what a weasel would look like up close, but the only face I could bring to mind was Darcy Dixon's. I had a vision of a weasel dressed in a pin-striped suit. He was sneaking along the wall of the hen coop, carrying a set of blueprints under one arm. He climbed up beside one of the hens and began to explain to her the advantages of zero lot lines and low maintenance. He was showing her the details of the model suite: breakfast-room and patio, broadloom throughout, ensuite bathroom . . . I was sure she was happy where she was, but she was listening to him, her head cocked to one side. I couldn't believe it. He was going to make the sale.

"Don't buy it!" I shouted. "He's a weasel! Don't buy——"

KABOOOOOM!

I woke up.

Don turned on the light. He was talking to me and pointing to a hole in the wall, but I couldn't hear any-thing. The air was full of blue smoke and acrid-smelling cordite.

It was a weasel all right. We identified it, using dental records. The hens sustained three more casualties, whether from enemy action or friendly fire it was difficult to say. This morning, they were all interred under the apple tree with full military honours in a service attended by all staff.

There was one other casualty. I'd forgotten that Freddy's truck was parked on the other side of the hen coop. The blast from Don's shotgun flattened both front tires and I notice the radiator is now empty. I said I thought my insurance would cover it but Don isn't so sure. He read somewhere in the fine print of my policy that the com-pany will not assume liability for acts of war.

August 12

The pace has been blistering and it has taken my mind off condominiums, politics and everything else. After four solid weeks bringing in hay we went straight into the harvest without a break.

It has been stinking hot and muggy. Men, machines and animals are reaching their limits. Well, maybe not the animals. Mortgage and Feedbin haven't put in a full day since the first of May. When you get this bone-tired, the only relief comes when a machine breaks down. We had a good one today.

Don and I were baling wheat straw in my front field yesterday with his ancient McCormick baler. I realize this compromises my earlier pronouncements about machinery and the old ways, but there is no older way to bale straw than with Don's McCormick baler. The forks on the roller in front pick up the straw, and an arm and a plunger do the rest. The arm pushes the straw into the chamber that makes the bale. Then it pulls back, and the plunger comes from the front to ram the bale, six inches at a times, out the chute at the back.

It goes, "Runch, crunch. Runch, crunch. Runch, crunch."

Don likes to tell people that his baler has broken fewer than ten bales in as many years, and he was warming to this theme once again when we paused at about four o'clock to adjust the string tension.

He pulled the power take-off lever to start us up again and there was a great ripping "sproing" from inside the machine. We both jumped back out of the way and watched from a safe distance as pieces of metal flew through the air. The arm and the plunger were out of sequence, both trying to ram at the same time.

"Stay put, Walt. This could get ugly."

The two arms smashed away at each other, pounding the machine without mercy, until the main gear was whizzing freely in the air, and the baler lay in a crumpled wreck. When Don thought it was safe, he slipped in behind the tractor and shut it off.

"You okay, Don?"

"Jeez," he said, "did you see that? Did you ever see a machine commit suicide like that?"

I confessed I hadn't.

"Well, to hell with it," he said. "Let's get cleaned up and go to the dance."

Every August, the Women's Auxiliary gets together and holds a dance to break up the harvest. They hire a one-lung orchestra from Lavender and wax the floor of the Orange Lodge for the occasion. A general amnesty is declared on Catholics and the pictures of King Billy crossing the Boyne are retired into the loft to avoid offending anyone. Half the community sits on a single row of squeaky folding chairs along the wall and listens to the band play through its entire repertoire twice—that's four tunes altogether. Meanwhile the other half stands in the parking lot outside and talks about crops and politics. After an hour or so, people start dancing.

I strolled out to get some air after the first set of square dances and found the boys sitting on the bumpers of a couple of trucks, smoking and drinking from stubby Coke bottles. Jimmy beckoned enthusiastically.

"Come here, Walt," he called. "You look like you been rode hard and put away hot. Have a cool drink."

"Just what I need. Thanks, Jimmy."

I had a long pull out of the Coke bottle and it burned all the way down. I coughed and handed the bottle back.

"Jimmy, you shouldn't be drinking this stuff."

I looked over at Freddy, but he grinned and said, "He's just had a couple, Walt. He's all right."

Jimmy pranced around the truck, holding the bottle high in the air and singing:

"Oh whiskey, you're the devil,
You're leading me astray . . ."

I leaned back against the truck and watched Jimmy whistling and shuffling in the gravel. The crickets were singing at high pitch, and every so often a truck whizzed by in the darkness on the highway. A cool breeze lifted the leaves of the horse-chestnut tree beside us, bringing with it one of those strange premonitions of summer's end.

"Naw, there's no back-hoe work over there," Freddy was saying. "He's got a couple of fellas up from the city with a flat-bed truck and two machines. I go over to ask him why he don't use a little local help and he tells me I should clean up my front yard. Called it a junk-heap. I told him, I says, 'It'll be a junk-heap to you until the day you come lookin' for a carburettor off a '62 Chev.' It takes a long time to build up an auto-parts business like I got."

"I don't like it," agreed The Squire. "You know that field out behind the construction? First off he rented it back to Calvin Currie for twenty bucks an acre but now he's gone and offered Calvin thirty bucks an acre to leave it alone. Told him not to farm it at all. Damn waste of land."

I jumped in: "And he tells Don not to spread manure until the fall. Now do you see why I'm running for office? You can't protect your right to farm unless you are represented on council. That's the way a democratic system works. You've got to have a voice in order to change things."

There was an awkward silence and I was beginning to think I'd said something wrong.

"Running for council isn't the answer," said Don, finally. "Look, Walt, we probably shoulda told you. You haven't got much of a chance."

"Why do you say that?"

"Now, d-d-don't take offence, Walt," said Freddy. "It's not that people wouldn't agree with what you have to say. It's just that you're from the city. They won't even consider you."

"That's right," said The Squire. "A fella lost the last election up here because his wife's grandmother was born south of Highway Thirteen."

"You got about as much chance as a toad on the freeway," said Don.

"But you're right about one thing," said Freddy. "We've had just about enough from this D-D-Dixon fella. It's time we loosened his bolts a little."

Then The Squire said: "Jimmy had the right idea last spring, runnin' him off the road like that. Didn't make a proper job of it, but it was the right idea."

Jimmy was singing again:

"Ten years ago, on a cold dark night,
There was someone killed 'neath the town-hall
light . . ."

"Now look, fellas," I said hastily. "Let's not get carried away. If you want to stop Dixon you have to figure out how to keep people from buying his condominiums. He'll finish one unit, invite a bunch of high-powered real estate people up from the city and then do some selling to finance the construction of the rest. The only way to discourage him is to figure out a way to turn those people off."

"Well, how would you do that, Walt?" asked The Squire. "They're gonna be real nice houses."

"And you can't b-b-beat the neighbourhood," said Freddy. "If you had the money and didn't have to farm, where else in the world would you want to live?"

I laughed. "You may be surprised to hear this but there are some things about life in the country that people from the city have difficulty getting used to."

"Oh, you mean c-c-cluster flies. Don't like them myself."

"Snow's bad in the winter," observed Don.

"Can't get CBC up here," said The Squire.

"Well . . . that's partly it. But there are other things as well."

Someone announced the draw for the door-prize and the men moved towards the hall, leaving me alone with Jimmy and the first faint glimmerings of a plan. Jimmy was sitting on the truck tail-gate, singing at the moon in his tremulous tenor.

"And they shot 'em in pairs,
Comin' up the stairs . . ."

"C'mon, Jimmy," I said. "Let's go in. You've had enough."

Jimmy swung off the tail-gate and came around to the front of the truck. He surveyed me solemnly, took a deep breath and said, "I'll come in with you, Walter . . . *if* you can put my hand down on the hood of this truck."

This was ridiculous. I couldn't arm-wrestle an eighty-five-year-old man. But Jimmy grabbed me with his gnarled old hand and mashed my arm down flat on the hood of the truck.

"Do you dance, Walter?" he asked, twirling away again.

"Sure," I said, feeling my bicep. "Waltz, tango . . . listen, they're playing a foxtrot. Why don't we go in?"

Jimmy listened. "Sure and it's no foxtrot, Walt. That's the Little Burnt Potato."

He shuffled his feet and a cloud of dust rose around his boots. It took me a minute to realize that he was step-dancing to the music inside. He put his hand up on my shoulder and I found myself hopping up and down, trying to keep up with his footwork. His eyes shone with a combination of delight and Crown Royal and by the time the band reached the final chorus, we had heel-and-toed our way to the front door of the hall. Jimmy waved cheerily and tottered into the crowd, to join a square of people half his age.

I leaned against the cool cement-block wall to catch my breath, laughing to myself and listening to the crickets' furious singing.

August 27

The morning of Dixon's great condominium opening happened in the middle of what Don refers to as "the dead of summer," on one of those endless hot and muggy days, when everything has stopped growing and the whole township has turned brown. After chores I stepped up into the hay mow to make reconnaissance with a pair of binoculars. All the leaves had dropped from the Siberian elm in the heat, giving me a clear view of Persephone Glen. Everything seemed ready. Bunting fluttered from the sign. Lawn-sprinklers shimmered over the square of fresh green sod around the model suite. I'd almost forgotten what green grass looked like. The parking lot was freshly gravelled but still empty.

According to Dixon himself, seventy-five of the most influential real estate people from the city would soon be here. Waiting was the hardest part. The minutes ticked slowly by.

In my front field, facing the condominum, stood an ancient threshing machine, of the kind you see in pictures of the prairies before the Depression. It had been sitting unused in Freddy's driving shed for about twenty years but Freddy promised me that it would run. Beside the thresher was Don's massive John Deere Model "D" tractor and a hay-wagon neatly piled with sheaves of wheat. Jimmy was standing guard with a pitchfork.

They appeared on the horizon right on time. BMWs, Mercedes, Audis . . . ladies in pink and turquoise dresses emerged from the cars, stretched in the morning sunlight and wandered towards the model suite. From my vantage point I could hear the shrill "Howarrryaa!" and "Hi Guy!" . . . familiar mating calls of the male and female real estate salesperson.

By eleven o'clock, the parking lot was full of cars, the men were talking together in groups on the front lawn and some of the women were wandering along the side of the road, picking wildflowers. I spoke into the walkie-talkie.

"All right, gentlemen. This is it. Let's move that stock!"

It all started very quietly. Don and The Squire opened their barnyard gates. Holstein cows spilled out onto the road on the right, and sheep on the left. Now, there's nothing odd about a few sheep on the road . . . or a few cows. But two hundred sheep and seventy-five cows trying to pass one another on what is, after all, a very narrow road, can make the competition for wildflowers pretty intense. I could hear Don and The Squire cursing each other, just as if it had been an accident. Slightly ruffled, and perhaps taken aback by the colourful phraseology, the line of pink and turquoise dresses scampered back to the safety of the lawn and resumed their conversations. We had them now. They would be there, quite literally, until the cows came home.

Again I spoke into the walkie-talkie: "Very good, gentlemen. The pincer movement seems to be working well. I think we can move to Phase Two now."

The Squire disappeared back up his lane. Don sauntered easily through the front field to the thresher and swung up onto the John Deere. The tractor went "Rrr . . . rrr . . . whooosh, thoop-thoop-thoop." Don pulled the power take-off lever. The long belt between the two machines started to move and the thresher came to life. Jimmy climbed onto the wagon and forked the first sheaf onto the conveyor belt. The thresher bit into the sheaf with a great whine and a clatter and belched a golden shower of chaff out through the blower. For a moment, Jimmy and the thresher disappeared, but then reappeared as the golden cloud drifted slowly towards the model suite. Another sheaf went into the machine. As I watched through the binoculars, Dixon stepped through the patio doors and reached for his phone. Then my phone rang in the stable downstairs.

It was Darcy. He wanted to know what the hell was going on.

"We're threshing today, Darcy," I said innocently.

"Why can't you do it some other day?" he demanded.

"Oh, can't do that, Darcy," I said. "Gotta make hay while the sun shines."

"Can't you do it more quietly?"

"More quietly? Gee, I don't know. I kinda think if you could do it quietly they wouldn't call it threshing. Tell you what. I'll ask the boys to hurry things up a bit."

That seemed to satisfy him and he hung up. I went back up the stairs and picked up the walkie-talkie again.

"Freddy! Willy! Dave! Squire! Let's give the place some atmosphere!"

Freddy came roaring out of his lane on his big red Nuffield, hauling a manure-spreader brimming with a fresh load from the feedlot. Right behind him came three more tractors and spreaders with The Squire, Willy and Dave. Each of them had gone to some trouble to find a full load, representing a complete selection from the barnyard. They wheeled into my front field and criss-crossed in front of Persephone Glen, spewing chicken, cow, sheep and pig manure in all directions.

This aroma is not just offensive to the nose. It grabs lower down. What appears to the eye to be clear air, the lungs will simply not accept.

Dixon clutched the iron railing on his patio, a handkerchief over his face. His guests were falling back inside now, seeking the shelter of the air-conditioning.

My phone rang again. I picked it up on the ninth ring and, before I got the receiver to my ear, I could hear Dixon's voice.

"For God's sake, Wingfield! That smell is awful!"

"Smell?" I said. "What smell? Oh, that! Gee, I guess we get used to that up here, Darcy."

"One of my guests just threw up on the carpet!" he shouted.

"That's a shame. We'll certainly have to ask the boys to stop. I'm a little busy . . ."

"Tell them right now!"

"Okay, Darcy. No need to shout. Bye-bye."

Upstairs I gave the final order into the walkie-talkie: "We have them treed, gentlemen. Turn up the heat."

The boys abandoned the spreaders and converged on the thresher. Jimmy leapt on the John Deere and pulled the gas lever all the way back. The threshing machine went through an awful transformation. I knew it hadn't been oiled once in this generation, but, even so, the noise it made was incredible. It shrieked and banged and shook like a demented dinosaur. Then Freddy, The Squire, Don, Jimmy and the boys, all started feeding it wheat sheaves at once. The chaff boiled out of the blower, filling the air with a dust cloud so thick that the very sky went dark. I could no longer see the model suite. In fact, I couldn't see anything.

My phone rang once again. This time, we could hardly hear each other.

"Hello! . . . Hello? . . . Darcy? Gee I can hardly hear you."

"What the hell are you doing over there? My air-conditioning has broken down. We're suffocating in here!"

"I got the boys to speed things up, Darcy," I shouted. "They say they'll be finished by nightfall. That's too bad about your air-conditioning. That's a brand-new system, isn't it? Do you think something might have got in it?"

At this point Dixon sounded as if he was chewing on the receiver and I wondered if I might have gone too far. I tried sympathy.

"It must be hot in there with all that triple-glazing and no air-conditioning. I'd get it fixed right away, if you can find someone up here who knows anything about those systems. Listen, Darcy, I'd love to talk but I gotta run. Bye now."

I hung up and scampered back upstairs for another look. Suddenly, the barn timbers creaked and the feed-room door swung shut downstairs. For the first time in weeks, the wind was picking up. Today of all days. The dust cloud lifted from the model suite. Worse than that, I could now see that the threshing machine had spooked the sheep and cattle and they had returned to their pastures. Even if the wind died again we were running out of sheaves. The threshing machine banged and shuddered and stopped. I looked up out of the hay-mow door and was horrified to see blue sky and fluffy white clouds.

The patio doors on the model suite opened and people stepped back out onto the lawn. I heard a cheerful laugh. The party was starting again.

"Damn!"

Well, there was one last chance. It was an operation I had code-named "Canada." I knelt down beside Spike, taking his head in my hands and speaking into his good ear:

"Go on, Spike. Get down there. And remember, we're counting on you."

Spike floundered down the feed-room stairs. I hauled on the rope to the stable door where the Canada geese had been penned for the last two days on short rations. They were ravenous. They exploded out of the pen and struck out across the field, with Spike woofing behind them. At the fence they took to the air, caught sight of Darcy's lawn, the last square of green grass left on the Seventh Line, and descended on it.

They'd never been shy, those geese. After they finished the lawn they started on the hors-d'oeuvre. One of them even bit through the phone wire. I've never seen a plague of locusts, but if you ever need one, and you can't lay your hands on enough locusts, I recommend geese.

In a few minutes it was all over. Car doors banged, engines roared and the parking lot emptied, leaving Dixon standing alone on what used to be his lawn, shaking his fist at the geese.

We were all sitting in the hay mow, enjoying a beer after the battle, when the figure of Darcy Dixon appeared at the doorway.

"Golly, Darcy," said Freddy, "it's real nice of you to come over to help. But the truth is we've just finished for the day. Grab a beer, why don't you?"

The Squire said: "We had a pretty fair day, Darcy. Got a lotta work done. How did you do?"

"Hey, Darcy," said Willy, "did you hear about the Newfie who had ten kids and didn't want any more so he bought a condominium? Heeyah, heeyah!"

Dixon stood for a moment, glaring at us, and his gaze came to rest on me.

"Wingfield," he declared, his voice thick with rage, "I'll sue you, I'll sue the whole lot of you."

"For what, Darcy?" I asked. "For farming? It's all in the agricultural code of practice. I checked."

"We'll see about that. My lawyers will call your lawyers in the morning." He turned, took a step to go, but stopped and turned back to me. "Well, what about those geese?" he demanded.

"Those are wild geese, Darcy. I don't control the wild-life around here."

"Ain't it lovely, Freddy," said Jimmy in his sweetest voice, "the way the wildlife's comin' back. You never used to see geese around here."

Darcy turned on his heel, tripped on the door-sill and left. I followed him to the door and watched him stalk angrily down the gangway, his black leather shoes slipping on the dry grass, making a dignified retreat almost impossible. Chuckling, I turned back into the mow and found my neighbours all lined up in a row, waiting to shake my hand.

August 28

The morning after the Battle of Persephone Glen, the heatwave broke. Just before dawn I rolled over in bed and heard the first pit-pat of rain on the roof. It's a wonderful moment when you are wakened by that sound, look at the clock and realize that whatever was planned for the day is now cancelled.

I got up, headed down to the barn with a copy of the *Free Press and Economist* over my head to keep me dry and did the chores. Then I rode into Larkspur and did a leisurely crossword over breakfast at the Little Red Hen Restaurant.

After breakfast, I went into the General Store to pick up a few things. Mrs. Lynch was at the counter and Dry Cry looked up as I walked in.

"A couple of pounds of three-inch ardox nails, please, Mr. McKelvey," I said cheerily.

"I'll be with you in a minute," said Dry Cry shortly. "Did you find the cornflakes there, Mrs. Lynch?"

I picked up a brochure on steel siding and listened to the conversation with one ear.

"Just went out like a light, so he did," Mrs. Lynch was saying.

"What was it, do you reckon?" said Dry Cry.

"Hard to know. Just worn out, I guess."

"When did they say the funeral was?"

"Friday."

"Funeral?" I interrupted. "Whose funeral?"

Mrs. Lynch turned to me, her hand at her mouth. "Oh my goodness, Mr. Wingfield. Didn't you hear? Jimmy Bremner died last night."

"Jimmy?" I said. "That can't be . . . I was talking to him yesterday . . ."

"Oh, yes, it was very sudden," she said. "Mr. McKelvey was talking to Freddy this morning. They say Jimmy wasn't feeling well after supper and went to bed. When Maggie went to wake him this morning, he was gone, poor thing."

"Not much of a surprise, if y'ask me," said Dry Cry. "Seems to me he's been kinda overdoin' it lately."

The words stung. I stepped outside onto the verandah. It had stopped raining. All I could think of was Jimmy sitting on a hay-bale in the barn the afternoon before, laughing his head off about the geese. He'd seemed fine.

On the way home, I stopped Feedbin at Freddy's gate and looked down the lane. There were several cars in front of the house, so I turned in. Freddy was on his way to the barn with two milk pails, but he turned back and came towards us. He was brief.

"G'day, Walt. We're a little late with the chores, here."

"I just heard about Jimmy . . ."

"Yeah. Maggie tried to call you but there was no answer."

"What happened? Do you know?

Freddy shrugged. He seemed almost impatient. "Doctor had a look at him and said he didn't know. Just worn out, I guess. I better slip along and get these chores done. Maggie's in the house."

He trudged off to the barn. I would have gone in, but I thought Maggie would be busy with people and, rather than disturb her, I just went back to the farm. During the day I tried to keep busy but nothing worked. I tried to fix some fence. I tried to rehang the barn door but ended up sitting in the hay mow, looking out over the barnyard. That evening after supper, the phone rang. It was Freddy.

"Walt? We're giving Jimmy a bit of a wake here. Why don't you slip on up?"

I knew the whole community would be there. They always tell you exactly what they think and it wouldn't be any different this time. I got out my blue serge suit, dusted off my black shoes and walked up through the fields. Freddy was standing alone among the cars in the lane. I could hear the hum of voices coming from the front room. Freddy looked at my suit.

"Funeral ain't till tomorrow, Walt. You didn't need to get all dressed up."

"Oh," I said, feeling a flush of embarrassment. "I thought I should put on a tie."

"You look good, Walt." Freddy grinned. "How are you doin'?"

"Oh, Freddy," I said, the words coming in a rush. "I'm so sorry. I had no business letting him do so much with the horses. I just forgot that he was so old . . . and all that business yesterday——"

I didn't get any further. "What are you talking about? Walt, don't you ever think that way. Maggie and I have been sayin' all day that he's lucky he had you and those horses. The doctor said this morning he'd never seen Jimmy lookin' better. Which was kinda odd, considering he was dead and everything. But I knowed what he meant. Jimmy did look good. He'd quit the booze, he was eatin' his meals and takin' an interest in things. For once in his life, he was havin' a good time."

"He was?"

"That's right. Everyone in there's been sayin' it's a wonderful thing you did for him, Walt. He had the b-b-best year of his life, taggin' around with you and them horses. Now, come on inside. There's a bunch of people here want to meet you."

He was right. The kitchen was jammed with people and the noise was deafening. Someone stuck a beer in my hand and I found a spot near the egg-washer to sit down and look around. The table was covered with plates of cold cuts, pickles, breads and cheese. The sideboard carried industrial quantities of creamed Jell-O salad studded with pink and green marshmallows, jugs of pink lemonade and Freshie lined the counter and a big stainless-steel coffee urn chugged away by the sink. The day's rain had brought the flies inside, but the heat from the stoves kept them up on the ceiling. The hum of twenty-five conversations washed over me in gentle waves and I sipped on the bottle of beer.

"Are you Walt Wingfield?" someone asked.

I stayed late, met fifty people, talked about inflation, axe handles, the gold standard, whipple trees, treasury bills, the hole in the ozone layer and the rising price of beer. We talked about Jimmy, too. One old guy told me Jimmy talked to him about me all the time. In fifty years of knowing Jimmy he'd never seen him laugh much but in the last year or so the mere mention of my name was enough to set him off. He said he wanted to come out to the farm some time and meet the horses. That would be fine, I told him. I've been laughed at by the best.

I squeezed my way out onto Freddy's verandah, finally, thinking about Jimmy's wheezy laugh. I took a deep breath of the cool night air, watched the moon rise over Maggie's hollyhocks and drank a silent toast to Jimmy.

We'll miss him.

THE SECOND YEAR

house, show us how we made it. There's a bunch of people
here want to meet you.

He was easy. The kitchen was jammed with relatives and

A NOTE FROM THE EDITOR

I was at the funeral the next day. The crowd was so big
they had to put a bunch of us infrequent flyers downstairs
in the church basement. I hadn't been down there since I
was in Sunday School, but nothing had changed. The kids
were still putting up the same follow-the-dot pictures of
Jesus Christ on the wall.

The next day, Walt withdrew his name as a candidate
for Persephone Township council and, to everyone's surprise, he was replaced by Don. In October, Don got
elected and the first thing he did was appoint himself to
the land division committee that reviews all applications
for development. When it snows, Walt, Freddy, Willy and
Dave and The Squire all take turns calling him to get
their lanes ploughed out.

Darcy Dixon's condominiums drew about as much interest that summer as the Orangemen's Parade. By the fall he
still hadn't received a single offer and one day he just gave
up. He sold the property—model suite and all—to Walt.
Then he drove south and we never saw him again.

Walt had an auction sale for the model suite. Dry Cry
got his pine table back, for seventy-five dollars. Maggie
bought the triple-glazed windows for her new greenhouse.
There were no bids on the air-conditioning unit, so Freddy
hauled it back to his junk-heap, or I should say, his front
yard. He said you just never know when air-conditioning
might catch on in the country and if it did he wanted to
be ready with spare parts.

Willy and Dave made a bid on the structure itself. They

stripped the roofing, siding, eaves-troughs, verandah and plumbing out of it and started a whole new business. Now Willy takes the trees down and Dave follows right behind him, doing building repairs.

The geese flew south.

I was out there during the mail strike, just after Christmas, picking up one of Walt's letters, and I stopped for a moment beside the pasture to look at the scene. There was still no snow and the bare concrete walls stuck up out of the ground like an ancient fortress. They had begun to acquire the serenity and majesty of a Mayan ruin, and I began to understand what Walt meant when he said:

"When I came here, this was a sprawling civilization. But with my bare hands, I turned it into a wilderness."

THE THIRD YEAR

ANOTHER NOTE
FROM THE EDITOR

No one has been doing well out of farming the past few years. But Walt had more reason to be grouchy than most. By sticking to the farm the way he did, he missed out on the longest, sustained, stock-market rocket-ride of the post-war era. While his colleagues on Bay Street were lining their pockets, Walt prepared for his third profit-free season. We all told Walt not to take it personally. We reminded him that he'd always said the old ways were the best, and the one thing we all remember about the old days is that there was never any money around.

But Walt did take it personally. By the next spring, he wasn't talking about Thoreau or Montaigne or anyone else in the philosophical line. What reading he had time for tended towards the practical: farm papers, bulletins from the agricultural department and anything else that offered ideas for making ends meet.

He was starting to grow his own theories without help from anybody else.

Anybody who listened to Walt that summer would have realized how distressed he was by the gap between the theory of farming and the general practice of it. It was a gap he was determined to bridge even if he had to reform the whole system of agriculture in the process. That sounded reasonable enough to the rest of us. So we just got a good seat and settled down to watch what happened.

Dear Ed: March 22

Maggie tells me that whatever the weather is on the first day of spring, that's what you get for the next forty days. Yesterday was the equinox and I made a note in my journal that a cold northeast wind was blowing snow in off the lakes. If we get another forty days of this, these few sheets of paper may be the last word you hear of this expedition. I have never eaten a sled dog and hope I don't have to start with Spike.

The neighbourhood is deserted this week because the boys have all gone off on holiday for the March break. Don and his family went to the Bahamas, The Squire went to Florida, Willy and Dave went to Las Vegas and Freddy took a horse to the races in Buffalo. They've never all gone off at the same time before because one of them always had to stay behind to do the chores. They invited me to go with them, but I couldn't afford a holiday the way the farm is right now. I think they knew that before they asked me, and were hoping I'd look after things. It's just a matter of breaking a few bales open in the barnyard at Freddy's and The Squire's, but Don is milking fifty Holsteins and it takes a few hours. This afternoon I started for Don's barn a little earlier, since it was my regular night for dinner up at Freddy's.

I was flattered when Don first entrusted me with this responsibility, but then I found that Don's barn is so highly mechanized, a six-year-old could milk the cows if he could reach the buttons. I pushed a button to start the stable-cleaner, another button to start the compressor, one more for the silo-unloader, and yet another for the stereo system. Don says he has a pitchfork around somewhere, but I've never seen it. Hearing these familiar pre-supper noises brought the cows coughing and blowing to their feet. I guided the electric feed truck down between the mangers and gave each cow its ration according to the instructions on pieces of notepaper stuck to the beam above each stanchion. Then I lugged out the three milking machines and a pail of disinfected hot water and started my rounds. I like simple repetitive tasks. It gives me time to think, and these days, I have a lot on my mind.

The stock market is finally on its way back down and Alf Harrison is carrying out one of his Stalinist purges at the firm. On my last visit, he told me that the part-time arrangement we have is on hold until the market recovers. It wasn't a good day for him. I was late for the first-quarter sales review because my cows were out.

"Go play farmer for the summer," he said, "and tell me in October what you're going to do with the rest of your life. And leave that dumb hat at home the next time you come down for a board meeting."

He's got a point. I do have to decide where I belong. I like the life here all right but it seems that trying to farm these days means taking a vow of poverty. Especially the way I do it. Until I can put myself on a self-sufficient footing, I really can't begin to look at this as a permanent venture.

There is some force out there that seems to resist every effort I make to do things in an affordable, sustainable way. My instinct tells me that I'm doing the right thing by using my own labour and other natural sources of energy. Rather than look elsewhere for man-made solutions, I believe the answers should be found right here on the farm. The natural world is very unkind to what the business world refers to as the economies of scale.

Take a field of corn, for example. Nature doesn't like a whole field of one thing, so it sends weeds and bugs in to enrich the cultural mosaic. The farmer sprays the weeds and bugs and Nature starts building better weeds and more-resilient bugs. Before long, the farmer is spending so much on weapons that it ceases to matter if he wins the war or not. There is no profit left.

I try to farm in a way that Nature doesn't notice. I do many different things on a small scale, rather than one thing on a disastrously large scale. I call it the shotgun approach. My neighbours call it scatter-brained. I think I'm doing the right thing by obeying Nature's rules. The trouble is, Nature isn't paying my Chargex bill.

Don's farm is prosperous because he works in a closed system. He operates under the protection of the Milk Marketing Board, which provides him with a steady market and a guaranteed price as long as he meets his annual quota. The rest of the Seventh Line looks like Tobacco Road because we all operate in the open market, without quotas or protection of any kind. As Freddy says, we're the only businessmen who buy retail and sell wholesale. We'd like to be dairy farmers like Don, but the only people who can afford to buy dairy farms right now are rock stars and Mafia chieftains. Even if I could get my stock out of McFeeters, Bartlett and Hendrie, which I can't, it still wouldn't be enough to build a set-up like this. And Don himself complains that, although he's a millionaire on paper, the only real money he'll ever see will come when he gives up and sells out, which isn't much comfort.

By six o'clock, the milk was safely in the tank, the milkers washed and hung up, the cats fed and the all-night Barry Manilow tape was playing the cows to sleep. Since it was Thursday night, my regular night for dinner at Freddy's, I went straight there and tapped at the door. Maggie came out and opened the summer kitchen door but left the screen door closed between us.

"Hello, Walt," she said. "How did you make out at Don's?"

"Oh, fine," I said. "I've got it down to a science now. Are you going to let me in?"

Maggie frowned. "I guess I didn't expect you," she said slowly.

"Well, if it's not convenient, we can make it another night."

"It's not that it's inconvenient. I just didn't expect you . . . you know, this week."

"What, with Freddy away?"

"Yes," she said, still standing behind the screen door. I was beginning to feel awkward.

"Is there a problem?" I asked.

"People might talk, Walt."

"About what? What's the scandal? We're both over twenty-one and unattached."

"Well, exactly," she said and gently closed the door.

This was a first. After two years on the Seventh Line I thought nothing could surprise me. Spike and I looked at each other but he was not an expert on Persephone Township's rules of purdah. He whined and sat on his tail. Eventually we set off for home and canned spaghetti.

I don't know why I have an urge to make sense of things around here. Nobody else does. Freddy practises seven different trades besides farming and there still isn't a gate on the place that swings on its own hinges. Across the road, The Squire is sitting on land that goes up in value whether he farms it or not. He's waiting until land hits $5 thousand an acre and then he plans to sell out and move to Florida. Don's farm is prosperous because he has a contract with a marketing board. But that little piece of paper is now worth more money than his land and buildings put together.

And here am I, farming with machinery I got out of the dump and a horse that's older than my bank manager. If I spend three days at the firm in the city, I come home with more money than the farm will make all year. That makes the least sense of all.

How this country manages to feed itself is beyond me. I'm going to bed.

May 3

Maggie's prediction that the wind would blow northeast and cold for forty days has proved inaccurate. It is now forty-three days. But the time has come again for spring planting and I have been considering the prospect with a heavy heart. Last week, I went down to the barn and found Feedbin grinning at me through a hole she had kicked out of the wall with her hind feet. She was describing the view to the east to her stable-mates. I sighed and looked out at the drying fields, thought of the welded implements, riveted harness and life-threatening situations that lay ahead, and made a decision. I decided to buy a tractor.

I could have gone to my bank in the city, I suppose. My banker, Ed Edwards, has taken care of me for years, and we know each other fairly well. But he never has been keen on this farming idea and all I have to do is tell him I need a loan and the alarm bells will ring. If I land back in the city without a dime some day, it would be nice to have a bank manager who remembered me from my early, prosperous days.

So, this morning I went into the Larkspur bank to meet the manager at ten o'clock. I was directed to a cubicle without a door just off the main foyer of the bank, which struck me as a very public sort of a place for a financial conversation. A tired-looking man of about fifty-five rose, shook my hand and introduced himself as Mr. Moodie. He must have sensed my apprehension because he smiled apologetically and said: "Don't worry, they can't hear us."

"The door was a problem," he explained. "When people came in to make a big deposit they wanted the door wide open and when they were behind on a payment they wanted the door shut. Might as well put up a sign, eh? But with the door taken right off nobody knows what we're talking about. It's a lot more private. Now, what can I do for you, Mr. Wingfield?"

I explained that I needed a loan to cover the purchase of a tractor.

"Mmm-hmmm. We get a lot of people in this time of the year with plans for the season. I'm sure we can help out. Any idea how much money you're going to need?"

"Well, I was thinking of a used machine," I said.

"Something in around ten or fifteen thousand dollars?"

I must have turned white. I certainly hadn't been thinking of that much money. At the rate I was going, the next ice age would arrive before the farm paid back fifteen thousand dollars.

"How much income are you getting from the farm now, Mr. Wingfield?" asked Mr. Moodie, pouring me a glass of water from the pitcher on his desk.

"Not very much, that's why I'm here."

"Not very much?"

"No."

"Well, how much then?"

"Ah . . . virtually nothing, in fact."

"I see. How about from other sources?"

"I have a partnership in a brokerage firm in the city but my interest is locked in for the moment. They aren't paying me anything and they can't release my share right now, the way the market is. Just a temporary situation."

"Mmm-hhhmmm," he said with slightly more emphasis on the hhhmmm. "Still, if you have some collateral at the farm, machinery and equipment, livestock, that sort of thing . . ."

He must have seen the expression on my face as I thought about the prospect of listing a pile of antique implements, old King, six retired pigs and four Jersey cows as collateral. He leaned back in his chair and cocked his head to one side, deep furrows lining his forehead.

"You have the old Fisher place, don't you, Mr. Wingfield?"

"Yes, I bought it two years ago when the Fishers sold

out. That's when I left the brokerage firm to take up farming full time."

He'd heard about me. We talked about the farm and the economy and the weather for quite a while without any reference to my loan application. The hour hand on the wall-clock was coming around the eleven when he leaned forward, straightened the pens on his desk-set and frowned.

"Now, let me get this straight," he said carefully. "You have no income and no collateral and you haven't made any money out of the farm for two years and you want me to lend you fifteen thousand dollars?"

"I guess that would be a problem for you."

"No . . . no . . . ," he said slowly. "It's a pretty standard request around here these days."

"What sort of procedure do you follow in these situations?"

His pale blue eyes seemed to be reading something about four inches behind my head. It struck me that this was not a man from whom any secrets are hidden.

"The procedure, Mr. Wingfield, is that I send a form to head office telling them you have livestock and machinery that will cover the amount of the loan in the unlikely event that you can't pay it back. Then we both hope like hell that you do pay it back." He leaned back in his chair again and gave me a faint smile. "Why don't you have a look around at the dealerships and the sales and find something you like. Give me a call when you want to make a deal."

"That's very good of you," I said.

"Well, I don't suppose it's that much of a risk. There's people worse off than you. But still, I don't know how you people do it."

"Who? Do what?"

"Farmers," he said, getting up and looking out over the window-sill at the main street, "You know, if the bank didn't pay my salary for two years, I think I'd quit coming in to work. But here you are, and lots more like you, ready to buy seed and start again. Got to admire that." He turned back to me.

"We'll say the limit is fifteen thousand, then? I'll draw up the forms, Mr. Wingfield, and you go shopping. Let me know how you make out."

This was proving to be a lot easier than I thought. I stopped in the doorway of the office.

"You wouldn't by any chance know an Ed Edwards at the Main Branch in the city?" I asked.

He thought for a moment, but couldn't place him.

"I don't hear from head office very much," he said wearily. "And I'd kind of like to keep it that way. Know what I mean, Mr. Wingfield?"

I knew exactly what he meant. I felt the same way myself.

May 10

Experience has been a stern teacher in my past ventures with livestock. Every time I think I'm on to a good thing, Nature intervenes and cleans me out. In the past two years, every animal I have purchased in hope and raised for profit has filled a pauper's grave. Pigs, ducks, hens, geese . . . Why doesn't someone just put wax in my ears or tie me to the mast? The only animals that don't die in debt around here are the sheep, which is odd because they were the ones people warned me about. According to the neighbours, sheep have the life expectancy of a ball-turret gunner in aerial combat. Dogs run them to death, wolves sneak in at night and kill them one at a time. They get stuck in fences, roll into holes and can't get up, they eat wild cherry leaves and keel over. Sometimes they read an old copy of the *Globe and Mail*, get depressed and just lie down and die.

The only financial relief from this sad business comes from two government programs: sheep-damage claims and wolf bounties. Persephone Township pays you for any damage a dog or a wolf does to your sheep and they still pay a bounty for a dead wolf. It isn't much, but some years it can make all the difference.

Maggie knows all about this because she's been keeping sheep for years and was the one who encouraged me to get started as well. But I listened to Freddy talk about the hazards of sheep-farming and wondered if it made more sense for me to raise wolves. That way we could take advantage of both programs simultaneously.

I remember that first summer when I joined the sheep association, subscribed to *The Shepherd's Quarterly*, sent to the agricultural college for manuals on shearing and lambing, trained old Spike to herd my chickens and bought a shepherd's crook.

By the end of the summer Maggie was satisfied that I was sincere and offered to set me up with a few ewes. She drove them over one day, let them into the old orchard and warned me that the warranty had just expired.

It was an odd feeling after hearing all those horror stories about sheep to know that six defenceless little critters were walking around under the apple trees with "Kill Me" signs pasted on their rear ends. I found it difficult to get into a good book after sundown, knowing that the plot for a Roman Polanski film might be in progress out in the sheep shed. Every morning, I opened the shed door and peeked in, braced for disaster. Finally Maggie made a suggestion.

"Either stop worrying about your sheep or get a goat, Walt," she said. "Goats aren't afraid of dogs, and the sheep stay quiet when they have one around."

That's fine for her to say. She's learned to live with them. But the trouble is, goats can't be fenced, they eat flowers, they make trouble with the neighbours, they smell bad and they have a poor reputation in literature.

"What about a cardboard replica of a goat?" I asked. "Would that do?"

Freddy drove over the next day and delivered the goat. It was sitting on the front seat of the truck, looking out the passenger window, quite calm and apparently enjoying her afternoon drive. She was introduced as "Mrs. Hand," after the lady who sold her to Maggie. She was a rough-looking character, with rheumy red eyes and a slightly crazed expression. I had a collar ready and a length of rope to tie her to one of the apple trees.

"No charge for the goat," said Freddy. "I'd d-d-drive a lot farther than this to get rid of a few more."

That afternoon, Mrs. Hand chewed through her rope, climbed over the rail fence and strutted off towards the house. Spike went tearing after her, eager to prove himself

in this first opportunity at real-life sheperding. Mrs. Hand turned and glared at him and stamped her foot. Spike ignored the warning and dived in for a snap at her heels. She stamped very firmly on his head. He yelped and rolled back out of the way, thought for a moment and then came back to me with the apology that he didn't "do" goats.

Mrs. Hand climbed into the maple tree by the house and stayed there for the rest of the day. She has been there ever since. She does come down at night when it's time to go into the shed, but most of the time she perches on a limb of the tree like a jaguar waiting for some unsuspecting dog to happen along.

Maggie was right. I stopped worrying about my sheep. Mrs. Hand watches over the flock by night and day and I couldn't be any more relaxed about them if they were all trained in Kung-Fu and carried .45 revolvers. Out in the forests of the escarpment, Mrs. Hand's reputation has spread through the wolf community, and the term "wolf damage" has taken on a new significance. Thanks to her my lamb crop has been just enough to pay the Hydro bill.

There are wide curves along the road to agricultural prosperity. This week I followed up an ad in the *High County Shopper* for electric shears and went on an excursion up into the swamp farms of Pluto Township with The Squire's truck. As it turned out, the shears were for people, not sheep, but the trip was not in vain. The owner was very eager to find a home for an oversupply of turkey chicks he had out in the shed at the back of the property. He said something about keeping "a step ahead of the turkey police," which I presume was one of those impossibly obscure jokes they enjoy so much up in that country. At any rate, he gave me a hundred and fifty chicks for the price of fifty. Eyebrows are settling back to normal on the Seventh Line, but the smell of disapproval is in the air.

I lost a duck this morning. It was a year-old Rouen drake who has gotten into the habit of launching himself off the pig feeder whenever I come down to the barn. Usually, he just flies a few feet and lands on the stream but, this morning, a gust of wind caught him and sent him in a wide arc around the orchard and back towards the barn. I could see he was out of control and I shouted at him to pull up, but it was too late. He hit the side of the barn with a sickening thud and a puff of duck feathers. I put him in the freezer and posted a warning to the rest of the flock about unauthorized solo flights. The Flight Safety Board is investigating the cause of the crash.

May 17

When I announced my decision to buy a tractor, I expected to hear jeers and laughter and a chorus of I-told-you-sos from the neighbours, but I was wrong. They thought a tractor was a great idea. They handed me copies of the *Auction Register*, the *Woodfield Advertiser* and the *High County Shopper* with likely candidates circled in red ink. Freddy encouraged me to shop at home, pointing out that he had almost all the parts for a 1958 International, but Freddy says "almost" when he's collected four good tires and a steering-wheel. Don took me to see a man about a Massey 35 with three-point hitch, a loader and a snow-blower, but it was too expensive. The Squire spent a day driving me around to look at other possibilities but that confused me more than ever. Did I want a loader? Did I want three-point hitch? Did I want power-steering, power take-off, multi-power . . . ? I told them I just wanted a tractor that would pull things. I didn't care what the power was as long as it wasn't horse-power.

I took Feedbin for a ride to clear my brain and rethink the whole idea. We cantered through my field across the road, right out to Calvin Currie's place on the Town Line. Sitting out by the road in front of Calvin's house was a very simple-looking tractor with a fresh coat of green paint and a "For Sale" sign on it. Feedbin stepped gingerly through the ditch and approached it nervously, flipping her ears back and forth and whooshing through her nostrils. A voice called from the verandah.

"How are you now, Walt?"

Calvin Currie ambled over and held Feedbin's bridle while I got off to look more closely at the machine.

"Nice paint job," I said.

"You lookin' for a tractor, Walt?"

"Yes, I've been thinking seriously about it."

"I guess you'd know more about horses than you would about tractors, wouldn't you?"

"Yes, and I know very little about horses," I confessed. "Can you tell me something about this machine?"

"This here's the first tractor I ever owned, Walt. It's the 'AR' model John Deere. Used to be hundreds of them around this country. Sort of like the Model T of the farm tractors. Gas-powered, two-cylinder, stick clutch, and about thirty-five horse-power . . ." He paused.

"Is that it?" I asked. This was the shortest sales pitch I had heard yet. "So, what does it do?"

"Do? Why it pulls things, Walt. That's all it's meant to do. Pull anything. Cultivator, wagon, spreader, stone boat . . ."

Calvin handed the reins back to me, climbed up on the tractor and pushed down on the starter plunger. The engine went "Rrr . . . rrr . . . ka POW!! . . . clank . . . thoop . . . thoop . . . thoop-thoop-thoop . . ." Feedbin shied a few steps but came back, intrigued.

"The old John Deeres always were good to start," said Calvin. "And they're no trouble. I've had her forty years and she's never had a wrench inside her."

"Forty years?"

"I mind the day my dad brought her home. It was hot and I'd been rootin' up the summer fallow, ridin' the cultivator all day behind those damn horses. The sweat ran off 'em like a warm rain and when they switched their tails it came right back in yer face. Between that and the flies you had to shut yer eyes and let the horses steer. Well, when I seen this tractor I took the harness off the horses and threw it up in the loft. Never got it out again. Some people say they miss the horses, but not me. I couldn't wait to be rid of them."

I explained that I was approaching the same point myself and asked how much he wanted for his "AR."

"Well, Walt," he said, rubbing his nose and looking at the sunset. "I'll have to get what I paid for her."

"What, from forty years ago? How much was that?"

"Five hundred bucks."

So much for depreciation. Mr. Moodie would be very pleased. It certainly was a simple, solid machine. I studied the engine as it thooped away, noticing that all the engine parts were made out of cast iron. The part numbers were stamped on them in relief for easy reference. All the gauges still worked. The mud-guards were made out of quarter-inch steel and the gear-shift moved through a maze of channels to find the home of each separate gear. It was a very spartan machine without any options for the comfort of the operator. No cigarette lighter. No radio. Not even an arm-rest. Just the tractor seat and even that was removable for those who prefer to stand. Calvin let me take the tractor for a spin around the lawn and when I came back I wrote him a cheque on the spot.

"She pulls a little to the left," said Calvin as I prepared to depart, "and she throws a bit of oil, but she's got all the power she had in 'forty-eight."

"Thanks. Do you have any pointers for driving?"

"Just keep her between the fences, Walt."

I drove home around the side-road, with Feedbin tagging along behind on the lead rope Calvin had thrown in with the deal. He was right, the tractor did pull to the left. There was one complete turn of free play in the steering-wheel, which made navigation difficult. It was a bit like sailing in heavy seas, trying to correct gently as we drifted into the centre of the road and then spinning the wheel madly in the other direction as the bow finally answered to the helm and we veered back towards the ditch.

We made it home in one piece. I parked the tractor in the hay mow and put Feedbin away in her stall beside the others. Then, in a ceremonial fashion, I gathered up the harness and lugged it upstairs to the loft of the stable, just as Calvin and his father had done forty years before. The horses looked at me reproachfully but I avoided eye contact. I looked in on the turkeys before turning in and found that two had joined the feathered choirs. I pulled them out and set them on a barrel, ready for morning service under the apple tree. Then I returned to the house, where I spent a restless night, dreaming about horses that ran on gas and machines that ate hay.

May 24

The trouble with switching from horse-power to mechanical power is that all the implements have a different hitch. I now find that none of my horse-drawn equipment will hook up to the tractor. The morning after I got the tractor home, I took a saw and shortened the tongue of the cultivator and made a temporary hook-up with a chain and some black wire. By ten o'clock I was out on the top field with the cultivator bouncing violently behind but scratching up the soil with some success. Once the front wheel started following a furrow, the tractor travelled in a straight line and I didn't have to touch the steering-wheel at all. The wind was still raw and cold, and black smoke blew back in my face as I laboured up the hill alongside Don's cornfield. Don himself appeared at the crest of the hill, going in the opposite direction, with his big yellow Minnie and about sixty feet of disk ploughs behind him.

He did a double-take when he looked over and saw me. Then he lurched to a halt, jumped out of the cab, peered at the "AR" and made his way over the slabs of dirt and sod to the fence.

"Where in hell did you get that?"

"I bought it from Calvin Currie yesterday."

"You bought it? I thought you were gettin' a tractor."

"It's an old John Deere. You have one, too, Don."

"It ain't forty years old and it ain't the only one I got. Why didn't you get three-point hitch like I told you? It would do more for you, like run a snow-blower or a post-hole digger. That there's just a power plant."

That's Don for you. The slave of the industrial economy.

"The Squire says I should stay home when it snows and read my bible, and you can't dig a post-hole around here in any month with a vowel in it anyway," I said primly.

"Suit yourself," said Don. "Nice paint job." He returned to the Minnie.

Up at Freddy's at lunch-time, I got a more enthusiastic response. He greeted me in the laneway with a big grin and shouted his approval over the thooping of the tractor.

"G-G-Gollies, where did you find her?" He climbed up beside me and pushed the stick ahead. The tractor coughed and leapt forward.

"Watch it," I said. "The clutch is a little jumpy. Calvin Currie had it on his front lawn. He painted it last winter and just put it up for sale yesterday. It runs fine, except the steering's a bit loose."

"Loose?" said Freddy cranking the wheel around. "You sure it's hooked up at all? . . . Oop, there she goes." The front tire narrowly missed a fence-post. Freddy stood on one of the foot-brakes and the tractor whirled back around in the other direction, missing the fence-post once again.

"Golly! Brakes and everything. Yer all set."

"You think it sounds all right?"

"She needs to be tuned up. One of the cylinders ain't

firin' right. Must be a dirty plug. Let's pull 'er over here, Walt."

He wheeled over beside the hay-wagon. Just at that moment, Willy and Dave drove in, took one look at the tractor and immediately offered their assistance. As I listened to the conversation I began to fear the worst.

"Hey, Uncle Freddy, what's the gap for the points on this thing? You got the book?"

"They're all the same. S-S-Seven one-hundredths. About the width of a dime."

"Haven't got a dime. I'll have to eyeball it."

I went over to the barn where Maggie was working with her sheep. It's a bank barn, dug into the side of a sandhill, out of the wind, and the pens are warm and dry. The pens are laid out perfectly and they come as a bit of a shock, considering the general state of the rest of the farm. When I opened the half-door, there was a scramble in the main pen, and a row of sheep faces peered over the edge of the partition. Maggie was kneeling in one of the side pens beside an old ewe that reminded me of my Latin teacher at school.

"Here's a new lamb," she cried. "The last one of the season." Her face softened as she picked it up, still damp and wearing a dark patch of manure on its flank. She put the lamb to her face and breathed it in.

"I love the smell of them," she said and held it up to me so I could sniff it, too. "They smell like popcorn, don't they?"

It's a funny thing, but three years ago I would have said it just smelled like poop and asked her to take it back. Instead, I found myself sniffing gingerly at a spot near the lamb's ears. It smelled fresh and brand-new, which of course, is what it was. If the breath of life has a smell, this was it. "Popcorn? I haven't been to the movies lately, but you could be right."

"Why, Walter. Are you asking me to go to the movies with you?"

"Well, why not? We could take Lamp Chop with us and see if anyone notices."

"Walt?" Freddy's voice interrupted us. He was standing at the half-door, his hands covered with grease and his face as grave as a surgeon coming from the operating room.

"Walt," he said, "she's throwin' oil and there ain't enough pressure in them cylinders to b-b-blow up a balloon. If I know Calvin, she ain't had a wrench inside her in forty years."

Maggie and I followed him back across the barnyard where we found that the tune-up had progressed beyond the normal replacement of plugs, points and condenser. The tractor was up on blocks now, with the wheels off and green engine parts scattered about on the hay-wagon.

"It seemed to be running fine this morning, Freddy," I said. "It just pulls to the left."

"We'll fix that for you, too."

"Why don't you lend Walt the Case, so he can get back on the fields?" suggested Maggie. "I have to go into town to meet Sid."

"Guess Maggie told you she's thinkin' about a business, did she, Walt?" asked Freddy. "As if she didn't have enough to do around the place."

"Like what?" asked Maggie evenly.

"Like m-m-ministering to the needs of the suffering humanity around you. Ain't that good enough for you? You want to be a rocket scientist or something?"

Maggie turned back to me. "I'm opening a store down in Lavender with an old friend from school."

"What kind of merchandise are you thinking of?" I asked.

"Fabrics, dress-making sundries, patterns and that sort of thing."

Freddy sniffed. "There's no need for it when you look at

all the stuff Dry Cry has on the second floor. Heck, you couldn't chase a cat through it with a broom."

Maggie turned on him again. "If you like dressing up in a feed sack it's just the place. But the rest of us have to drive to Barrie for something to wear."

"Makes a lot of sense, Freddy," I said.

"You see, Freddy?" said Maggie.

Freddy didn't see. "What time will you be back?" he asked grumpily.

"Don't worry. I'll be back in time to minister to the needs of the incapacitated humanity around me."

Getting a tractor going at Freddy's is a matter of Byzantine complexity. To start the Case tractor, which is a six-volt, Freddy had to jump-start the Nuffield first, using the Pontiac. Once the Nuffield was running, he hooked up to the Case with a chain, pulled it a few feet while Willy let out the clutch and bump-started it to life. Finally, Freddy ushered me to the driver's seat like a head-waiter.

"Now when you stop, p-p-park it on a hill like I showed you before. Oh, and take my cultivator home with you. We'll rig a proper hook-up for yours in the next couple of days. You don't want to p-p-plant anything yet anyway, with the weather like this."

"Sure, Freddy," I said. "Thanks . . . and, by the way, who is Sid?"

"You never met Sid? I guess you wouldn't have, he's been away for a bit."

"Where has he been?"

"Workin' in the city since he got his finance degree, just like you, Walt."

"I don't have a finance degree, Freddy. I did ancients and moderns before I took the stockbroker's course."

Freddy looked puzzled. "I thought you went to university," he said. "Anyways, Sid knows business and he's got her all cranked up about makin' a million. He figgers the way she works, she'll make more money in a month than this farm makes in a year."

I was back on the field that afternoon. This time when I passed Don, he was making a final pass with the harrows before seeding. He recognized Freddy's tractor and cultivator and I could see him putting two and two together. He shook his head in resignation and carried on. I drove in monotonous circles in the cold wind for the rest of the afternoon.

June 1

The next morning at 9:45, the wind changed around to the southwest, and by 10:00 the temperature had risen fully thirty degrees. We went from winter to summer in fifteen minutes. I missed spring. I was inside washing the cream separator.

Four more turkeys had conked out, which meant another burial party under the apple tree and a later start for the fields. When I went out to bump-start Freddy's Case, it rolled all the way down the lane to the barn without firing once. We came to rest beside old King, who was standing in the shade of the apple tree, examining a bug on the ground. I sat there fuming, wondering how to get the tractor back up the hill, when old King lifted his head and nickered at me. It sounded like someone shovelling at the bottom of a deep well. I was about to return to the house and call Freddy when suddenly I had a brilliant idea. King would pull the tractor back up the hill.

King is a draught horse, but he has one large drawback. He does not respond to conventional horse-motivating words like "giddyup." In fact, you can't drive him with the lines at all. When I brought him home from Freddy's that first summer and hooked him up, I clucked and chirped away but there was no response. I went up to the engine room and looked him straight in the eye, searching for signs of mutiny. His expression was as amiable as Brian Mulroney's. The problem seemed to go beyond ordinary balkiness. To make sure, I took up the lines again, leaned forward and slapped him on the hindquarters. King turned his head slowly around and gave me a look of such mournful reproach, I never thought of doing it again. Since then, I have led him everywhere by the halter, which makes it impossible to handle an implement at the same time. However, he isn't bad at a dead-slow pull with a chain, for hauling a log out of the bush or one of the other horses out of the stable.

At any rate, I got off the Case and climbed up into the loft of the stable, to retrieve the single set of work harness. Feedbin and Mortgage exchanged knowing glances. When King saw me return, lugging the harness, his eyes brightened and he lumbered over to me. He even dropped his head to let me put the collar on him.

I tied the steering-wheel to the seat and looped the drag chain in a knot around the front axle. Then I went back and rooted around through the empty beer bottles in Freddy's tool-box, looking for a piece of wire to secure the chain. The tractor suddenly jolted forward, away from me, and I looked up to see King, head up and motoring, dragging the tractor off after him. For one terrified moment I thought I had another runaway.

"Whoa!" I shouted. King stopped and his head dropped down to ground-level again. I was speechless. What on earth had made him start by himself? I thought back carefully through my last movements. Then I went to the tool-box and rattled the beer bottles. King's head flew up, he leaned into the collar and the tractor lurched forward again at about one mile an hour.

This was amazing! He was going in the wrong direction, towards the barn, and I had no lines to steer him with, but at the rate he was travelling, I had plenty of time to think back to the days when Jimmy was working with the team. What would he have done? What was it he used to yell at them? Besides the other stuff . . .

"Gee!" I shouted. King tilted to the right like a battleship and we began a wide right-hand turn away from the barn.

"Gee," I shouted again and the scenery continued to rotate. I untied the steering-wheel and let the wheels follow around afrer him. At the top of the hill by the house I tried "Haw" and got a perfect left-hand donut turn. The tractor was now set for another run down the hill. I unhooked King, asked him to stand to one side, let off the brake and trundled down the hill again on the Case. It gave a couple of "pitoos" but failed to catch and we came to rest beside the apple tree once again. This time, I just turned the key off and gathered the beer bottles out of the tool-box. King and I were going back to work.

Well, the news travelled quickly and by the time I had my old cultivator readapted for horse-power, the whole neighbourhood came down to see King in action. Freddy finally cleared up the mystery.

"I made a call to Sarnia, Walt," he said. "Got a hold of the fella who sold him to me. Seems K-K-King was the last milk horse in Sarnia and the fella who drove him got tired of the school kids takin' off with him. So he trained King not to move when someone said 'giddyap' and the like. But when he g-g-give the milk bottles a shake, away he'd go."

This discovery about King has been something like finding the cruise-control switch on a car you've been driving for a year. It is a liberating feeling to have a horse that actually works for a living. The Case is still sitting by the apple tree and who knows when the green machine will return from the repair shop. But for now, I'm not worried. I'm sitting under the maple tree on the line fence, watching King cultivate the field by himself. I just have to shout "Haw" at him when he gets to one end of the field and back he comes. As long as he stays within earshot I have complete control. Don passes by with his corn-planter on the other side every so often, but he is pretending not to notice. I don't know why he's being so competitive. He could work up the state of Nebraska by the time King and I finish this field.

But I can see now that, this year, I will get it finished. More importantly, when my field is planted, my invest-ment will be my time and nothing else. Well, King's time, too. In the end, Don and I will get the same crop, but the difference is, I haven't spent any money. That really should be the first rule of farming: Don't spend money.

Now if there were just some way of extending that rule to other parts of the operation.

June 15

Something is rotten in the turkey shed. This afternoon the body count rose to eight and I called the vet in Larkspur. He said it sounded like coccidiosis. I had heard this diagnosis before and remembered the treatment. Four milligrams of sulphur dioxo . . .

"Did you say you've got a hundred and fifty of these birds?" the vet asked. "I'll be out there after supper. I'd get some help if I were you."

When The Squire arrived, I asked him what kind of help I might need.

"Once they start goin'," he said, "you need a good man with a shovel."

Freddy agreed. "I never had any luck with them."

"Can't we do something?" I asked.

The vet moved through the flock slowly, stooping every so often to pick up a slow bird and hand it to me. A turkey brigade formed and we separated the sick from the flock and deposited them in an infirmary in the other barn.

"Just have to pour the antibiotics into them and hope for the best," he was saying. "Avian diseases are tricky. By the time you know what strain it is, half the flock's gone. We'll send one down to the agricultural college at Guelph for a report. Should know in a few days. You got quota for these birds?"

"Quota?" I asked.

"If you have more than fifty turkeys, you're supposed to buy quota. That's the law."

Before I could answer, The Squire spoke up. "This is a kind of a co-op here. Each of us has fifty birds and Walt feeds 'em for us."

"Well, it's none of my business," he said shortly. "Anyway, if this keeps up you won't need anything, except maybe a back-hoe. I'll give you a call in a few days."

I didn't like the sound of this.

"Quota?" I said, after the vet left. "Nobody ever said anything about quota."

"Don't worry about that, Walt," said Freddy. "Have a beer."

"Am I going to have some marketing board down my neck because I don't have quota?"

I'm getting used to the fact that some of my questions don't get answered around here. I used to think maybe I might have said the wrong thing, but now I know it's just that the question has no answer, or it won't help me to know the answer. It's nothing personal.

But since we were in the rest period between spring planting and the first cut of hay, no one seemed to be in a hurry to get home. A case of twenty-four appeared and everybody sat down in the straw to watch the sunset.

"What's the field and crop report say, Willy?" asked Dave.

Dave shook out the *Eastern Farmer* and read aloud to us:

"The cool wet weather has not been conducive to field work or crop development. Corn emergence is very uneven, with zinc deficiency, sun scald and wet feet syndrome. The hay harvest is variable. Some producers are leaving big ruts just tryin' to beat the alfalfa weevil. Major fleabeetle problems continue in the Pine Valley areas."

"Just full of good news, aren't they?" said The Squire.

Dave continued. "The window for control of white winter wheat disease has now passed . . ."

"I'll sleep easier knowing that," said Willy.

"Most wheats are showing heavy mildew and septoria. Barley is yellow due to denitrification and wet feet. Weed escapes are general. It is another good year for rescue herbicides . . ."

And I thought "The National" was depressing. The conversation moved gradually into that incomprehensible twilight world of technicalities that all farmers and financiers seem to enjoy, except me.

I fell asleep.

No word from Guelph yet and the situation is still serious. The morning service under the apple tree is now a regular event. Seventeen turkeys have gone to their reward and I am poorer for their passing. The vet assures me that we will have the best scientific advice in another day or two. All I can do in the meantime is keep pulling the sick ones out when I see them.

But all is not doom and gloom. I had a lunch date with Maggie yesterday. Well, maybe I shouldn't call it a date. She was in town working on her store opening and I was at the library reading up on turkey diseases. We bumped into each other outside the Red Hen and she graciously consented to join me for lunch.

I certainly didn't intend to talk economics the whole time, but that's what we did. You see, ever since that afternoon in the field when the first inspiration hit me, I have been working on a plan that might restore some sanity to the economy around here. It all came bubbling out when I sat down to lunch with Maggie.

She listened to the whole thing and told me it made a lot of sense. She even thought the others would be interested in it, too. So I told her I was thinking about inviting the neighbours down to the farm on Thursday evening for an economics lecture.

She's a smart woman. She said if I made it an economics lecture and barbecue, people would come. She was right. On Thursday evening, The Squire was the first to arrive.

"I hear you've got something cooked up for us tonight," he said. "Hope it isn't one of your turkeys."

When Willy and Dave, Don, Freddy and Maggie turned up I made sure everyone had beer or lemonade and started passing hamburgers off the grill. Then I began my talk.

"For years now, the prices of farm inputs—land, machinery, fuel, insurance, taxes—have all been going up. In the meantime, the price of farm produce has remained the same and, in some cases, has even dropped."

"That sure is the truth," said Freddy.

"That gap means more than just thinner profits," I continued. "It also represents a growing disparity between the real value of your labour and the price you are able to command for it."

"What did he say?" asked The Squire.

"You have to work twice as hard to stay where you are."

"Yes, thank you, Maggie. You can see for yourself that things are completely out of whack when the price of land goes to three thousand dollars an acre, while the value of the crop you grow on it is only a hundred dollars."

"It don't make no sense," said The Squire.

"I've been thinking about this a lot and it strikes me that the problem is a matter of control over costs. The problem is that when we spend money, nine times out of ten the money leaves the community and never comes back. When we buy fuel or fertilizer, or make a mortgage payment, the money goes to some big company in the city and the only way it will ever show up back here is in the form of higher real-estate prices. These gains are illusory because they can't be realized."

"What did he say?" asked The Squire.

"He says the only way we ever get our money back is if we quit and sell," said Maggie.

"Thank you, Maggie. Now, Don here is doing as well as anybody because he works in a closed system, with the Milk Marketing Board. I believe we should think about doing the same thing as a group right here on the Seventh Line."

"What, you're gonna start yer own marketing board?" chuckled Don.

"More like a customs union," I explained. "We need to keep on producing anything that will generate cash from the outside economy, but we should have a formal system of barter among ourselves for subsistence items, to prevent cash from leaking out of our own community."

"What did he say?" asked The Squire.

"He's saying we shouldn't be paying cash for groceries when we can trade stuff around for nothing," said Maggie.

"We always done a bit of that," objected The Squire.

"Sure you have," I said. "But we can do a lot more of it so that no cash ever changes hands among ourselves. Our first rule of farming should be *Don't spend money.*"

Don shifted in his chair and leaned forward. "Who would keep track of all this?" he asked. "I got enough paperwork as it is."

"I've done the paperwork," I announced. "I want you to have a look at it and tell me what you think." With a flourish worthy of the boardroom I showed them an example of the new Seventh Line currency I had been working on the past few evenings. It is square, to avoid confusion with the Queen's currency, and it promises to pay the bearer, on demand, goods or services at the rate decided by the community.

I had printed one hundred and seventy-five units of the new currency and I proposed that each of us start out with twenty-five.

"So what are the income-tax people gonna have to say about this, Walt?" asked Don.

"Ah . . . I think we can all appreciate that there is a certain need for confidentiality here. Is that a problem?"

They all looked at one another and there was a long silence. Willy and Dave took the currency to the light and examined it carefully.

"Hey, Dave," said Willy, "it looks like the stuff you get at Canadian Tire. Only there's no picture on it. Shouldn't you have your picture on it, Walt?"

"My signature should be good enough. That's all the central banker does, usually."

"You gonna be the banker?" asked Dave. "So what do we call these things?"

"Walt printed them. We'll call them Walts," said Willy.

Maggie laughed. "What's a Walt worth these days?" she asked.

I showed them a chart with suggested rates of exchange. One unit of the new currency would buy an hour's labour, or three pounds of butter, or one rooster, or three dozen eggs or two quarts of fresh cream, and so on. As the central banker, my job would be to maintain the stability of the system by promising to redeem any or all of the units at the agreed exchange rates. Once we got going, I proposed that we meet once a month to review the rate structure and make changes if they were needed.

It's funny, but the whole thing went just like a board meeting down at the firm. You know how it goes. Someone makes a presentation he's been working on for months and after he's finished, the discussion goes back and forth like a free-range chicken. You never actually hear anyone say, "Approved." You just have to listen to the tone of the discussion to know whether the idea is going to fly. I think I knew for sure that we were in business sometime after ten o'clock when The Squire waved one of his Walts at me and asked:

"Hey, Walt. Can I get a beer with one of these?"

July 1

It has now been a week since the Walt was introduced and everything is going fine. I did a brisk trade in eggs, cream and roosters. I helped Freddy on the hay for a couple of days, The Squire hired me to replace some of the boards on his barn and Willy and Dave got me to make a few trades for them on the stock market.

Everyone covered his purchases with the new Walts. I was delighted. Even Don came over and offered me five Walts for a pile of cedar posts I had sitting beside the barn.

My turkeys are still in bad shape and the vet sent me into the Co-op with a new prescription for drugs and medicated feed. The men on the loading dock threw the bags into the back of The Squire's truck and raised this unpleasant business about turkey quota again.

"You want to be careful about the Turkey Board, Walt. They find out you got that many birds and no quota, the turkey police will be down on you like a duck on a June bug."

"Turkey police? You don't mean to say they actually have turkey police, do they?"

The expression on their faces said this was not a joke.

"But, we have a co-op arrangement. I'm feeding them for everybody on the Seventh Line."

They all burst out laughing. "That's what they all say, Walt. The Board doesn't buy that one any more. Better keep your head down."

While I was waiting for The Squire, I wandered into Dry Cry's store for a bag of fence staples; my only purchase from him this week. I was digging handfuls of staples into a paper bag when I was startled by Dry Cry's voice at my shoulder.

"Haven't seen much of the Seventh Line this week. Sure miss the business," said Dry Cry.

"I expect everybody's busy on the hay," I said, avoiding his gaze.

"I hear you got a scheme goin' down there for savin' money. Is that right?"

"You've heard?"

"Oh sure. I hear a lot of things. Printin' your own money and everything."

"Well, it's just a little experiment. We don't mean any harm by it."

"Of course you don't mean no harm. Sounds like a real good way to save a dollar. If my customers can figure out a way to save their money these days, I'd have to be a real hard man to stand in their way, wouldn't I?"

He was taking this all rather well. Over the next fifteen minutes, despite the comings and goings of customers he stood beside me and chatted as if there wasn't anything else in the world he would rather be doing. It was the longest conversation I have ever had with Dry Cry. We talked about prices and distribution and he agreed whole-heartedly with my theory about the barriers to prosperity that face the farmer.

I explained to him that he would eventually benefit from our scheme. "Sooner or later," I said, "no matter how much money we save, we'll be in here with it to buy something. You might lose a bit of business today but over the long run, you may even do more business."

"Now, that would be real nice. Say, can I see one of them?"

"What, a Walt? Well, sure."

I dug one out of my wallet for him and he admired it in the light of the store window.

"You're welcome to it," I said. "I'm very pleased

that you don't feel we're trying to take advantage of you."

"Of course not," he said with his face all crinkled up in a smile. This was a side I had never seen to Dry Cry and it made quite an impression on me. He was a lot nicer than I had ever imagined he could be and I'd found this out almost by accident, by taking the time to stop and chat with him. It all goes to show that we shouldn't be so quick to judge a person. You just never know, do you?

Back at the farm, I found Don sitting in his pick-up, waiting for me.

"Got any more posts?" he asked. "I could use another fifty and I can't get at my own."

"You mean, the ones in your swamp?"

There is a cedar swamp that sits along our property line, mainly on Don's side, but it's hard to tell because it has never been fenced. It's hard to get at because the hill going down into it is about ten degrees too steep to negotiate safely with a tractor.

"Yeah," said Don. "You'd need a bulldozer."

"I might get them out with the team, I think."

"You call that a team?" he snorted. "You got two horses and neither one has the brains God gave a bird."

"That may be, but I think they'll pull those posts out. Anyway, if I do get them out, what's it worth to you?"

"Same as I paid you for these here," said Don. "In Walts, of course. But you're wasting your time. You'd need a bulldozer."

Next morning, I was down in the swamp bright and early, buzzing down every straight cedar I could reach. It was hot and very buggy, but by noon I had twenty good-sized trees felled and trimmed. After lunch I got the heaviest harness I own, trussed Feedbin and Mortgage together like a couple of kidnap victims and clattered off with them to the swamp, dragging a heavy chain behind us. They jostled and banged against each other, frothed at the mouth and stared wildly at the scenery as we made the descent. At the bottom, I looped the chain around the butt end of one of the trees and turned the girls in the direction of home. Then I unsnapped the lines from their bridles, stood safely to one side and yelled "Giddyap!"

Unreliable as these horses are, I knew that as soon as they were headed in the direction of the barn it would take more than an old cedar tree to hold them up. Heave ho and out they go! They went sailing up the hill like an artillery outfit in the Boer War. I jogged up the hill behind them and, at the top, I just stood and watched as they flailed home to the barn, with the tree bouncing along behind.

Persuading them to return to the swamp was the difficult part, but my luck and the harness held. They galloped home with three more trees. On the fifth trip home, they trotted. On the ninth trip, they walked. At the end of the day, two cross-eyed horses and a half-dead stockbroker were standing over twenty Walts' worth of cedar posts in the barnyard.

On the way into church on Sunday, Don took me aside and asked me if he might borrow my "team" some day. I sat on the hard bench, feeling quite pleased with myself and watched the rest of the congregation file in. Maggie appeared, looking lovely. She took her seat a few rows ahead of me on the other side of the church and I began concocting an elaborate scheme to trick her into another lunch date.

I was all set to doze off during the sermon, but the minister chose as his theme one of those commerce-and-finance lessons from the Gospel according to Saint Matthew. You remember, the one about the man who gives each of his servants a few talents? Just at the part where two of the servants were making daily compound interest, Maggie turned around and gave me a big smile that just lit up the church.

Back at home, I took stock of the situation. I was exhausted, my freezer was empty and one hundred and seventy-four Walts were back in my hands. That didn't bother me. After all, I'm playing the role of central banker and I know the importance of establishing public confidence in the new currency. For the system to work properly, they all must satisfy themselves that the Walt has real value. The acid test will come next week, when I go out into the market-place myself, as a buyer.

You know, Ed, I think Maggie really likes me.

July 10

The turkey situation is desperate. They are dropping like flies now and the vet has pretty much thrown up his hands. I've given up on the morning prayer service under the apple tree. I think I'm going to need a land-fill site. I got the old freezer in the garage running and started throwing the bodies in there until I get time to deal with them properly. It's very depressing. Whatever profit I might have made is gone now, and all I can hope is that enough survive to pay for the feed.

This morning I went off to see if my barter system would work both ways. My first visit was to The Squire. I asked him if he would part with some electric fence I needed for the sheep pasture.

"I'd give it to you, Walt," he said. "But the fact is, I don't have any. Why don't you try Willy and Dave? Oh, and how about some more of that cream?"

"Sure," I said, "but I can't barter with you unless you have some of the currency."

"Oh, I got some all right," he said, producing five Walts out of his top drawer.

That's funny, I thought. I was sure that all but one were back in my hands. I must have counted wrong. I carried on and found Willy and Dave driving cattle along the road. The grass gets very dry at this time of the year and Willy and Dave spend most of their time retrieving stock from other people's pastures. By September, they give up completely and cattle graze the ditches of the Seventh Line undisturbed. They refer to it as the "long pasture."

"Hey, Dave," shouted Willy through the dust. "We got any electric fence?"

"Hell no, Walt," replied Dave. "Why would we be chasin' cattle if we had a fence like that?"

"Say, Walt," said Willy, "we're havin' a chicken barbecue in a couple of weeks and we need about ten more of your roosters. Can you spare them?"

I repeated what I had said to the The Squire. Without the currency, we can't barter. To my surprise, he pulled a handful of Walts out of his back pocket and handed them to me. I must have flinched because Willy looked at me closely.

"You're still takin' these things, aren't you, Walt? I can still get a rooster for each of these?"

"Yes, of course," I said. I wondered what condition I must have been in when I counted those Walts. I folded them up and went straight to Freddy's. Don and Freddy and Maggie were sitting in the kitchen when I arrived.

"Hi, Walt," said Maggie. "C'mon in."

"I ah . . . was just wondering if anyone has any Walts left?"

"Yeah," said Maggie, opening her purse. "I got a few left here."

Don and Freddy produced five each of their own. That brought the total to well over two hundred Walts. I can't have been that far out. Something was definitely wrong.

"Do you mind telling me where they came from?" I asked, as calmly as I could. "I just like to keep tabs on things, you know."

"Oh sure," she said. "I got these from Dry Cry. He's giving them away at the store."

"Giving them away?" My voice was rising.

"Now, Walt, it's all right. Dry Cry said he thinks your idea is great. He's accepting the Walts at the store and, as a goodwill gesture, he's giving away a few as bonus coupons."

"Yes, but . . ."

Freddy was looking closely at one of his Walts.

"Say . . . is this your signature, Walt?"

"Oh, boy," said Don. "That skunk."

I slumped down at the kitchen table. Dry Cry! I should have known! By the end of the week, the Walt would be taking a beating against all other currencies and I would be fighting a losing battle against inflation. Heaven knows how many more of these things are out there. But this was no time for panic. The most important quality in a central banker is a straight face.

"Oh my Lord, what am I going to do?!"

"Don't worry, Walt. You leave this one to us," said Don.

A car horn beeped. Maggie scooped up her purse and headed for the screen door. "That'll be Sid," she said. "He's taking me in to the post office. I won't be long, Walt."

Freddy tipped his chair back and looked out the window as Maggie hopped into the car and banged the door shut. "So he still thinks that horn works as good as a doorbell. Mum used to hate that, do you remember, Don? Maggie always said he wouldn't come to the door because he was shy."

"How could you call a man shy when his car horn played 'Chantilly Lace'?" asked Don.

"Yeah. He had that 'fifty-two Monarch with a flathead-eight motor in it, bored right out. You know the ones. They had the big generator sittin' up on top of the motor, remember?"

"I saw one of those big flatheads in a gravel truck once," said Don. "You could spin the wheels in all four gears with a full load."

"Maggie and Sid went out together?" I said. "I had no idea. What happened?"

"You know how these things go, Walt. They never last. She rusted right out from under him."

"She what? No, no. Not the car. What happened to Maggie and Sid?"

"Oh . . . Sid went to college in the city and got a job down there. That was the end of it. Haven't seen him till this summer. Now he's back, it looks like he's ready to pick up where they left off."

"He is? They are . . . ?"

I heard a loud buzzing noise that sounded like a cicada in the tree outside the kitchen door, but it was actually coming from my own eardrums. For a second I thought I was going to faint. But I didn't. When my head finally cleared, I found Freddy and Don had returned to the subject of Sid's car and were trying to recall the firing order of a flathead-eight.

So Maggie has a beau. It had not occurred to me. How stupid of me.

"What does Sid actually do?" I asked finally.

"Same as you, Walt," said Freddy. "He's a financial planner."

I flinched. On Bay Street, the term "financial planner" has come to mean anything from "unemployed" to "on parole." There is no such profession, although thousands still travel under the title.

I put my glass down on the table and noticed a rather formidable legal-size document spread open in front of me. Maggie's name was on it. I looked more closely and realized it was the partnership agreement for Maggie's fabric shop. It was none of my business but I flipped over a page to the revenue-sharing section. After two paragraphs my alarm bells went off. I couldn't believe what I was reading. It was all done in percentages but cross-referenced back ten pages to the partnership agreement. I flipped back and forth four times, working out Maggie's share at different revenue levels. Each time, I got the same paltry figure. And the liability clause left her obligated for everything but her first-born child.

I have no idea how long I sat there, but when I looked up, Freddy and Don had long since gone and Maggie was standing in the doorway. I hadn't heard her come in.

"Walter," she said, in a puzzled voice, "what are you doing?"

"Well, I'm reading this contract, Maggie, and I suggest you do the same. I think the Better Business Bureau might have a look at it, too."

"What are you talking about? It's none of your business."

"It becomes my business when some huckster tries to cheat you out of your money."

"Hucks . . . ? How dare you say that about Sid! He's not trying to cheat me out of anything!"

"I don't know who your friend is, but if he wrote this contract he's a crook. Have you worked out your return on investment after the net-net-nets in this thing? Did you notice that your percentage refers to residue, not to the gross? And this liability clause is like something out of the Old Testament. I've never seen anything like it. Where did this man take his business training, on the Spanish Main?"

"Stop it! Stop it!" she cried. "It's not true. I won't listen to this. I think you're awful. The one chance I get to be happy and you want to spoil it all."

"I'm not trying to spoil anything, Maggie. I just want you to be careful. I'm thinking of your happiness . . ."

"No, you aren't. If you were you'd just leave me alone. But you can't. You can't stand to see anyone have a chance to be happy because you're a frustrated old . . . bachelor!"

She ran from the room, in tears. I sat there for a few moments, looking at the contract. Then I got up and left.

I stumbled down through the fields to the farm and spent the rest of the afternoon in the barn, sitting in the hay mow, looking out over the valley. At suppertime, I was reheating a tuna casserole of uncertain vintage when Freddy appeared at the screen door.

"Good news, Walt! Yer tractor's fixed."

I let him in.

"What have you got there?" I asked glumly.

He was carrying a cast-iron housing, which he set on the kitchen table.

"I dunno," he said. "We put her back together and this was left over. Don't think we should throw it out yet. So what's on your mind, Walt? You got a face as long as a wet week."

"I don't know, Freddy. My currency scheme is a mess and when people find out about Dry Cry's stunt, I'll be a laughing-stock. The summer's half gone and I haven't accomplished anything. My turkeys are a disaster. All I have to show for my efforts is a stack of money I printed myself."

"And you had a bit of a scrape with Maggie. I wouldn't worry about it too much, Walt. You'll get your feathers back."

"It's more than that, Freddy. I've got to get out of here before I do any more damage. Maggie's right. I'm just a frustrated bachelor, meddling where I don't belong. It's time I went back where I came from and forgot about this pathetically stupid pipe-dream once and for all."

"Walter, look. I know you're upset. But give yourself a little time here. You don't want to do something you'll regret later on."

"No, my mind's made up. Please don't argue with me. I'm going to phone Alf Harrison in the morning and tell him I'll be back in to work in a couple of weeks. So, I'll have to get things cleared up right away. Freddy, I want you to book me an auction date as soon as possible."

"Okay, Walt," said Freddy doubtfully. "If that's the way you want it. But folks will be real sorry to see you go."

Me too, Freddy. Me too.

August 7

I rose with a heavy heart on the morning of the auction and went down to the barn to do the chores for the last time. The animals must have known what was up. They stared at me in silence as I did the rounds.

Freddy and his team were in auction sale when I came back from the barn, pulling machinery into rows and piling odds and ends on the hay-wagon. I never liked auction sales much. It's so depressing to see a person's belongings spread over the lawn for the whole neighbourhood to pick over. It was worse today, because the possessions were my own.

The hay-wagon was parked in the drive and it carried the accumulata of the past three seasons: old harness, a chicken-feeder, a hog trough, rolls of wire, boxes of nails, staples, assorted tools, the contents of the medicine cabinet, the cream-separator, cream cans, feed sacks and a pitchfork.

My meagre collection of equipment was lined up along the orchard fence: an 1870 Oliver single-furrow plough, a disk harrow *circa* 1934, a cultivator (welded beyond recognition), a seed drill (old, but in working order), a hay mower (old, and not in working order) and a dump rake (from the dump).

People started to arrive about ten o'clock even though the sale didn't start till noon. However people seemed to be avoiding my company. I suppose that, when you leave, people do their best to remind themselves they never thought you'd stay in the first place. Freddy joined us and asked me one more time if my decision was firm.

"Walt," he said. "Are you sure you want to go ahead

with this? You know, everybody would understand if you changed yer mind."

"No, Freddy," I said, "it's too late for that. Go ahead, start the sale."

Freddy jumped up on the wagon and the crowd drifted over to hear him do the opening patter.

"Ladies and gentlemen, gather round and let me acquaint you with the terms and conditions of this sale. I have been commissioned to sell by public auction the effects of one Walter Wingfield of the Seventh Concession of Persephone Township, the sale consisting of articles listed in the bill of sale, which you will agree are too numerous to mention. If you are a successful bidder, please be so kind as to identify yourself to the clerk, speakin' of whom, I'd like to thank Henry here for standing in at short notice in this capacity today. The terms are cash, cheque or whatever arrangement you are able to come to with my clerk. Now, without futher delay, we will proceed to the first item and drive on. Henry, bring out Lot Number One."

At most farm auctions, the hay-wagon and machinery are sold first and the livestock is held to the end. That's because the livestock is considered the main attraction and a crowd won't thin out while there are animals waiting to be sold. In my case, Freddy decided to reverse the order, explaining that he thought some of my animals were so old they might not make it through the afternoon.

I knew it wasn't going to be easy, but the first animal brought out was old King. He blinked in the sunlight and stared at the crowd, sighed and his head sank to ground-level. I guess he knew all about auctions. The crowd laughed.

"Here y'are, boys, if the energy crisis comes back yer all set with horse-power and the Arabs can't touch you. What am I bid for this old fella . . . who'll say a hundred bucks? Whoolabidma-hundadollah-whoolabidma-hundadollah-hunda-dollah-andabidma-hundadollah-nobodybidma-hundadaLLAH? Well, say fifty and let's get started. Fifty-bid-an-whoolabidma-fifty-fifty . . . ?"

The crowd was silent. Old King examined a gum wrapper on the ground and remained motionless as Freddy worked the crowd but the asking price continued to drop.

"Fifty-five-fifty-five-whoo'll-tell-me-then-dive? . . . Fifty dollars? C'mon boys, you tell me what he's worth! Who'll tell me twenty-five . . . ? Say ten . . . ?" Freddy frowned. "C'mon fellas. Pick him up for ten dollars and you can sell him to Walt Disney for a thousand."

It was useless; there were no bids. They led King back

to his stall and returned with Feedbin and Mortgage harnessed together. I had warned Freddy this wasn't a good idea but one of his helpers claimed he could drive any team that could be harnessed. They came round the corner of the barn now on their hind legs, staring wildly and frothing at the mouth.

"Here's a good strong team, folks, broke to ride and to draw. Take notice now! Worked every day and lots of energy to burn. It took three years to break 'em in and it'll take ten to wear 'em out. Jeez, don't she buck! Keep them children back, Henry. We'll sell the harness separate. Who'll start me off at two hundred dollars for the team?"

A voice from the back said, "I'll give you five dollars for the neck-yoke."

"Well, all right. That's a start," said Freddy.

Just at that moment, Mortgage and Feedbin turned towards each other, flipped the neck yoke over their heads and headed back towards the driver. He dropped the lines and fled. The horses galloped off towards the stream, passing on either side of a butternut tree as they went, snapping the neck yoke like a matchstick. The crowd cheered.

Freddy shook his head. "We'll sell them if they come back," he said.

The Jersey cows came next.

"No, gentlemen, these aren't antelope, but here's your chance to own the last four Jersey cows in the county. Used to see them all over but hunters shot most of them, thinkin' they were deer. Who'll give me a hundred apiece for the Jersey cows?"

Freddy prattled away to the impassive crowd, but nobody wanted Jersey cows either. Freddy leaned down to me from the wagon and whispered, "I guess yer livestock's kinda exotic for these people, Walt. Sure you wanna keep goin' here? If you do, I think we better move on to the wagon and machinery. Crowd's gettin' restless."

I nodded and Freddy straightened up to address the crowd. "Gentlemen, this wagon is gonna go next. You see for yourself it's got good tires and a strong axle. Who'll start me off at five hundred for the hay-wagon?

One-hundred-anabid-fifty-anabid-wannabid-whooolgimme-fifty?!Whoool-say-forty-anabid-wannabid-whoolgimme-twenty-five dollars . . . ? Come on boys! What's she worth? Who'll say ten and let's get away? Hector, Walt paid you a hundred two years ago and it's got a new rack on it. Helluva way to treat a neighbour, folks."

The trouble was the wagon had been adapted for pulling by horses and it would cost as much to readapt it back to tractor work as anybody thought they might spend on a used wagon.

"Who'll say a dollar?" said Freddy finally. There was a long silence and The Squire finally stuck up his hand. A minute later Don raised the bid to two dollars. Then Willy and Dave took it up to four. Hector bid five and the bidding stopped.

"Sold," announced Freddy and Hector got his wagon back. Everyone except Hector looked relieved.

"You can see there's gonna be some bargains here today, folks," said Freddy, in the largest understatement of the morning. They moved on to the articles piled on the wagon.

Don bought the cream-separator. He carried it away, saying he could always plant flowers in it and put it on the front lawn. The Squire, who hasn't kept chickens or pigs for years, bought the hog trough and the chicken-feeder. Willy and Dave bought the cream cans.

I couldn't stand it anymore.

"All right, Freddy," I said. "That's enough."

He leaned down again. "What's that, Walt?" he asked. Everyone could hear us but, at this point, I didn't care.

"I said, that's enough. Stop the sale. This is turning into a tag day."

"People are just trying to help out," said Freddy.

"I know and I appreciate that, but I want it to stop. Just tell people to go home."

I turned and walked away, down the bank, past the barn and on through the fields. It was a still summer day and the heat rose up from the stubble in the hayfield as it would from a stove. Two large horse-flies flew in endless circles around my head as I crossed the fence and walked down into the flats along the Pine River. I took my shoes off at the river-bank, waded to mid-stream and sat on a large rock.

For the next half hour I tried unsuccessfully to drown a water strider by holding it underwater in a tin can. But it didn't work. I was just giving it up as a bad job when a voice spoke to me from the river-bank. It was Maggie.

"Hi, Walt."

She lifted her dress to the knees and waded out to the rock.

"I came to apologize," she said abruptly. "You were right about Sid."

"I was?"

"After what you said about the contract, I took it to the lawyers. They figured something was wrong and called Sid. He told them he'd explain everything but nobody's seen him since. He's gone."

"I'm sorry, Maggie. You must be very disappointed."

"Well, I should have known. Sid always was like that. I thought he might have changed. But there's no reason for you and me to fight about it."

"I guess not."

"You still planning to go?"

"Yes, I am. The community will have to look elsewhere for its amusement."

"They already have."

"What do you mean?" I asked.

"Willy and Dave found all those dead turkeys in your

freezer when they were setting up the sale. They loaded them up in the truck and dumped them on Dry Cry's front lawn."

"They did?"

"Mmm-hmm. Then they called the Turkey Board and told them Dry Cry's keeping birds without quota. The inspectors are up there now giving him quite a time."

We laughed together and I went back to harassing the water strider.

"It doesn't change anything, Maggie. I've made a mess of things and it's time for me to leave. I'm a failure as a farmer. I can't go on like this."

"You haven't made a mess of anything. Let me tell you something, Walter. You may not have noticed but, when you first came here, we were all sitting around looking over the neighbour's fence, wondering who was going to get the highest price for his land. Then you walked in and started farming like it was 1905. Sure we laughed at you. None of us thought the way we live made much sense, and we couldn't see any point in trying to turn back the clock.

"But you showed us that it does make sense, the way we all live in each other's kitchens, keep gardens, trade stuff around and help each other out. It scares me when I think how close we came to forgetting that.

"And the others see it, too. The Squire says he's changed his mind about Florida. He's having so much fun he wants to retire right here. Willy and Dave want to stay and farm. Don says he'll stay if the rest do. And you couldn't get Freddy off the place with dynamite.

"What I'm saying is, if you go now, it'll be a sad day for the Seventh Line . . . and for me, too."

"You, too?"

"Well, go on, Walt Wingfield. Let me make a fool of myself. I suppose it's better than waiting for continental drift to bring us together."

A FINAL NOTE
FROM THE EDITOR

The wedding took place in the Anglican church in Larkspur. Freddy gave the bride away and Alf Harrison came up from the city to be Walt's best man. Don and The Squire were ushers. Walt asked me to read a poem. It was a scene of great contrasts, that wedding. But everybody got on just fine.

Willy and Dave trucked old King up to the church with the buggy so Walt and Maggie could ride down to the farm together. But King moved so slowly, they had to truck him back again or the couple would have missed the reception.

The Walts gradually went out of circulation. It's not that we didn't trust them. I guess everybody had to have one as a curiosity, and before long they were all framed and hanging on walls across the township. They even got one up at the Revenue Canada office in Barrie.

Don started using Walt's team and by the time they got all the cedar posts out of the swamp, the horses had settled right down. Don kinda liked working with them. Of course, he hasn't given up any of his tractors yet and is still the "slave of the industrial economy," as Walt would say.

The Squire gave up his idea about Florida. He retired right where he was and rented the fields to Willy and Dave while they looked around for a farm of their own. It didn't take long. The boys sold short just before the market crashed and that winter they bought the farm off the plastic surgeon up the road. They moved out a few months after Maggie, and before we knew it Freddy got himself a housekeeper.

The turkeys didn't all die. Walt found some way to scratch up the loan payments before his money came in from the firm, and somehow he got a crop off that year to feed everybody through another winter. Maggie got the store going in Lavender after all, with help from Walt and another loan from the bank. Their problems aren't over, but he and Maggie get by, pretty much the way everybody else does on the Seventh Line.

The next year, the tax department did an audit on Walt and everybody else on the Seventh Line. But they didn't get a dime. Maggie was keeping the books.

And me? Every now and then I get a letter from Walt, but not that often. I don't print them any more; I just pop them in the drawer here. I guess he's so busy just living out there, he hasn't got time to write about it.

Which is a nice way to be, when you think about it.

ABOUT THE AUTHOR

DAN NEEDLES was raised on a farm near Alliston, Ontario, where he had animals and a garden to tend. He was also raised in a theatrical tradition: his father, William Needles, is a founding member of the Stratford Festival Company. Dan at first avoided both traditions, studying economics at the University of Toronto. In 1974, he became editor of the Shelburne *Free Press & Economist*, in which the original version of the Wingfield saga made its appearance. He was subsequently director of public affairs for an insurance company.

In 1984, the *Letters* became the basis of a one-man stage play, starring Rod Beattie, and Dan Needles became a playwright. Audiences across Canada have applauded some six hundred performances of the stage version and many more have enjoyed the episodes produced for CBC radio's *Morningside*. His latest play, *Perils of Persephone*, premiered at the Blyth Festival in the summer of 1989. Dan Needles now lives with his wife, Heath, and one-year-old daughter, Madeline, on a farm near Collingwood, Ontario.